TKITKITKITKITKITKITKITKI
KITKITKILIESKITKITKITKIT
ITKITKITKITKITKITKITKITK
TKITKITKITKITKITKITKITKI
KIMAKEITKITKITKITKITKIT
ITKITKITKITKITKITKITKITK
TKITKITKITKITKITKITKITKI
KITKITKITKITKITKGODSKIT
ITKITHETKITKITKITKITKITK
TKITKITKITKITKITKITKITKI
KITKITKITKOFKITKITKITKIT
ITKITKITKITTKITKITKITKITK
TKITKITKITKITKITKITKITKI
KITMONSTERSKITKITKITKIT
ITKITKITKITKITKITKITKITK

The
Koalemos
Initiative

A novella

P.H. Wilson

Dedicated to:

My Father:

Who never gave up on me and always pushed me to follow my dream.
May you rest in peace.

My Mother

Thank you for giving me life and a second chance at it.

Muse: Elle

Thank you for your inspiration. I shall never forget it. Nor you.

Foreword:

At the tender age of 10, I blindly picked up a pen and scrawled my first poem. I had no idea what I was going to write, but nevertheless there it was staring back at me, this quatrain that had poured out of me so easily, yet I had not consciously written. My muse was a young girl by the name of Jennifer Stewart, she sat to the right of me in Mr. Murphy's class. At the time I did not know the difference between love and muses, so of course I allowed juvenile infatuation to steal its way into my heart, not that I ever verbalised such notions, but still they blossomed into a majestic Sakura that would soon come to bear a host of false loves that were really muses in disguise. Where Jennifer Stewart ended up I do not know and I am certain she never thought of me, but she will forever be a part of me, for she is the key that opened the gnarled oak door that reads Poe deep with my soul. Many would say that I was lucky because I had a purpose, but a writer can barely make money in this era let alone a poet, so I struggled on for the next 24 years writing poetry and stories that have been rejected countless times. My ego spurring me on, trying desperately to cling to the vain delusion that fame and fortune will be mine with a single book, but that never came. I pushed forward anyway not contemplating that my rejections could be down to the simple fact that my writing ability is far from what is needed to reach the upper echelons of the literary world. I spent my days loathing every flavour of the month or the Hollywood blockbuster hidden in paperback form, then I met Hemingway and Kawabata. Those two changed everything for me. I saw the art for art sake and I lost the ridiculous notion that one had to produce two thousand words a day like I am no more than a factory mass producing shoddy goods for some low cost bargain store. James Joyce wrote a couple of words a day, so am I now meant to cast him aside because he does not meet some James Patterson level of mass production? No! Writing is art, writing is humanity and in the words of Hemingway "We are all apprentices in a craft where no one ever becomes a master." With that said, writer's have forgotten the ways of art and like art, writing is defined in styles not genres. We are simply in the midst of a movement we cannot see, trapped in its boundaries and prejudiced ideals.

The purpose of any and all writers is simple; we are but pieces of something greater. We are contributing to one great masterpiece that depicts the life of human beings. Shakespeare contributed a chapter, Hemingway, Kawabata and Steinbeck a page each. Camus and Lu Xun a paragraph while Stephen King has given a sentence or two. Myself? Not a word, because I was always more concerned with making a vast profit off my writing as if I were a pushy stage mother who curses her offspring for ruining her acting career. I spent far too much time reading through useless books produced by agents, or writers who never actually made it but wanted to cash in, on how to write a cookie cutter novel so that you too can sell your soul and fill the ever-growing void stealing literature's intellect, but after decades of it, I am finally done. I would rather be like Hemingway and Kawabata slowly crafting their works and not having much money, but still doing what compels them because no matter how much of a curse it is to me and no matter how hard it can be to get that perfect set of words on the paper. I love every second spent crafting my works. I love to experiment and play around with the nature of stories as well as how they are designed and if that means I am relegated to the independent press for the rest of existence, so be it, because I love writing and the threat of poverty and ultimately death no longer scares me, because if you cannot find something to live for, then you best find something to die for and in writing I have found something worthy of living for and something worth dying for.

Sincerely,
P.H. Wilson

开始

Yasunari Oda (1951-2011) was educated in Tokyo and at the Institute of Technology in Kyoto. In 1974, he quit his studies to devote himself to literature. In 1976, he wrote his first novel, which was not met with critical, nor financial success due to the avant-garde nature of the piece. At the age of twenty-seven, he was arrested for taking part in the Narita Airport protests. In 1989 he was released from prison and allowed to return to his writings. In the fourteen years before his death, Oda continued to promote his own genre of writing called philosifiction, which was never fully appreciated during his lifetime. Sadly Oda's existence and works have almost completely been erased from history due to heavy censorship and government denial.

F&K Books

Published by Fukushū and Koalemos Books

www.thekoalemosinitiative.com

馬鹿は死ななきゃ治らない first published in 2011
This translation first printed in 2017

The
Koalemos Initiative

Unedited and Uncensored

Yasunari Oda

Translated by P.H. Wilson

F&K

F&K Books

TRANSLATOR'S PREFACE

It has become quite common place in the translating of philosifiction to, for the lack of a better phrase, dumb down the source material, as well as fix all of the intentional grammar and spelling mistakes, however I have decided to limit this as much as I can so that the reader, who I, as well as Mr. Oda himself, have always argued is far more intelligent than they are given credit for. That said I must warn the English speaking reader that they may find some of the phrasing a little odd and this is down to philosifiction being a genre that is exclusively written in Japanese. Hopefully by using foreignization as my translation method I will allow you to better understand the allegorical nature of the work and see what Mr. Oda meant by his coining of the term philosifiction and the deep seated personal questions that are layered, sometimes quite thick, throughout his work. Also it should be noted that the "Author's Preface" is not meant to be understandable as it is a puzzle that you the reader must solve, so that you may begin your journey.

Sincerely,
P.H. Wilson

Author's Preface:

Tuqh huqtuh,

Mubsecu je co meha, Y xefu jxqj edu tqo oek mybb ru qrbu je iuu yj veh mxqj yj jhkbo yi, rkj veh dem buj ki wuj je jxu hyttbu oek qhu iuqhsydw veh. Zeosu edsu iqyt jxuhu yi edbo edu mqo je qsxyulu yccehjqbyjo qdt Y myix je juij jxyi jxueho, ie cksx ie jxqj Y qc mybbydw je fkj co emd ceduo ed jxu bydu, mxysx skhhudjbo ijqdti qj vylu jxekiqdt tebbqhi qj jycu ev fkrbysqjyed. Fbuqiu iuu jxu muriyju jxuaeqbuceiydyjyqjylu.sec veh vkbb tujqybi qdt hkbui.

Bqjyd xqi de ruqhydw xuhu qdt oekh mehti qhu dej jmudjo-iyn, Y vuqh. Q ckbjyjktu ev bqdwkqwui oek ixqbb vydt rkj ev jxi coijuho edbo Udwbyix sqd kdmydt. Veh kdbyau Ixqauifuqhu'i heiu, dqcui tuvydu jxyi fheiu. Beea je jxu iydyijuh qdt ev feujho'i ruqkjo oek ckij qtcydyijuh. Qdt jxuhu jxu qdimuh ixqbb ru qdt jxu jhku dqjkhu ev jxyi meha oek ixqbb iuu.

ACT I

Compendium Exordium

Onkunde

To read many books is harmful.

----- Mao Zedong

A miniature canary yellow bicycle splashes through the serene puddles lining the decaying asphalt, like a young child running along a sandy shoreline. The water droplets soar upward, spraying the worn frame with their cold merciless authority, the remaining globules, which sparkle in the midday sun, spatter against a pair of faded denim jeans. The world over is inundated with the intimate heartbeat that accompanies a steady rainfall. The screeching brakes of two high-end vehicles with fading bumper stickers, that suggest their owner's views are far from enlightened, shatter the windswept sidewalks. The bike weaves between the two automobiles, its worn treads gripping onto the slick pavement as best they can. The pair of irate drivers scowl at the dark haired man cutting through the traffic. The rider's hands clutch onto the handle bars like a trapeze artist set to take flight, while the bike itself hops onto the curb. The front wheel strikes a puddle and goes askew, pushing the cyclist toward a store front that reads "World's best bagels". The rider's trainers graze the window, patrons, who are awake enough, reel backwards. A man in the midst of a midlife crisis screams as his fresh brewed latte soaks into his Brunello Cucinelli jacket. The frigid downpour envelops the rider, while his mind drifts in and out of music blaring through earphones that hang from numb lobes. The strident rhythm and crushing bass caressing his senses allows his mind to become a voiceless entity that knows of the cold ravaging it, yet is far enough removed that it is but gossip in its eyes, as for the rider's, they are searching for Kensington Palace Gardens or as it is better known Billionaire row. The rider's gaze plunges through the broken promises and faltering residents. The white hot rage reserved for his existence is palpable. The only thing preventing him from bursting into a dazzling array of fiery orange and crimson red are the icy stares pointed in his general direction.

The rider gives those around him a fleeting glance. He sees an older couple chattering away. A single guffaw escapes the man's lips, his wife smiles at her husband's unbecoming laughter. That is until she sees the rider. Her liver spotted hand pulls at her purse. The cyclist shrugs this off as nothing more than the atypical behaviour of the typically behaved. The rider weaves in and out of two more sets of sidewalk dwellers then cuts his handle bars hard. A rainbow shoots out from the miniature typhoon sprouting from the back wheel, but fades within seconds of its birth. The tired sidewalk jockey passes the Russian Embassy followed by a private residence that is not as grand as one would assume. In front of the next overpriced home, a pair of men, who look like tuna stuffed in tutus, stand discussing the previous night's football results, only taking a moment's pause to unleash a cavalcade of fatuous comments in middle class French. The cyclist flies by without bothering with their contemptuous conversation, for whatever moronic thoughts the pair might share, the rider is safe in the knowledge that they are still nothing more than overpaid meat shields in undersized jackets. The rider eyes his target, his feet cease their peddling and soon his wheels rest against the entry gate. The chain that had clung to the conveyance's frame now hangs limply between the gate and the bike's back wheel. The cyclist pulls a medium Japanese style pizza, and the aroma of Shiso leaves that comes with it, from the pizza container on the back of his bicycle. The pizza man walks up the empty drive, his feet the only thing to touch its damp surface all morning. His gaze set upon a home that no sane being could justify owning, yet every government in the world could without question. With each step he takes, the world behind him vanishes, leaving him with the eerie silence that has ensnared the upscale community. His finger presses the ornate doorbell, a chime echoes throughout the house. The cyclist waits for someone to collect their order. A minute passes, and nothing. He pushes the doorbell again and waits for the absentee owners. "So bloody typical." The pizza man sighs, slamming his fist against the door. The black piece of varnished mahogany opens with a speed reserved for front doors being opened by cheating spouses at three in the morning. "Great! I'm either in a horror novel or a thriller. I hope to Anu it's horror, at least then I'll get to have sex before I die." The cyclist mutters.
The rider, going no further then the cusp of the entrance, shouts. "Hey

almost certainly dead owners and the sadists who caused their demise, I'm going to set this pizza down and sl…" Before the cyclist can finish, a figure dressed in black appears from behind the shadows and fires several shots. "Damn it, it's a thriller." The rider says flinging the box at the masked man. The flying piece of cardboard misses its intended target and ends up splattering, the culinary abortion within, against one of the meticulously maintained walls. The cyclist's pair of white shell toes clash with the marble floor while his legs piston forward in search of escape. His driving run is highlighted by the intermittent screeches of the assassin's Type 67 pistol. The rider dives into a room that prior to this moment had provided its owner with a place to read during the late afternoon hours. His rain slick form slides along the floor like a greasy bowling ball down a lane, but there are no pins to crash into, only a bookcase once owned by Emperor Taishō. Several pieces of the dormant fiction plummet to the ground. The pizza man tries to shield his body from the barrage, but gets struck in the head. The masked assassin's pistol gives a fleeting look to the blemished bookshelf then nudges downward to the pile of East Asian literature. A bullet fires from the silver cylinder and drills its way through the oak of a nearby desk. Before a second shot can leave the chamber, the pistol flies from the masked man's hand thanks to a dog-eared copy of "The Dancing Girl of Izu and Other Stories" by Yasunari Kawabatta striking his skull. The rider's legs push his body up from behind a chair celebrating its bicentennial. His brown eyes watch the military issued weapon tumble to the ground like a printer's matrix upon a molten sheet of metal. The assassin snatches at the tumbling firearm, but Newton's first law is having none of it and the metallic pistol continues its downward spiral.

The gun lands with a thud, wobbles for a moment then ceases. The rider's eyes fill with despair. The masked assailant reaches down and plucks the gun from the ground. His finger squeezes the trigger but a voice shouting out the name Li Jun stops the completion of this diabolical ballet. The assassin swings toward the voice only to be greeted with the sound of a weapon going off in rapid succession. The first of these bullets perforates the assassin's black turtleneck, the second his cheek and the third tears through his skull with such violent intent that part of his formerly brown eye oozes out of the rear of his fragmented cranium.

The pizza man catches sight of the vicious attack, his legs however, are another story. The two bodies collide in an array of death and adrenaline. The cyclist closes his eyes, grabs hold of the masked assailant's pliable frame and uses the dying man's withering form as a human shield. The collision sends the pair plummeting. Unfortunately for the pizza man, he takes the brunt of the fall. The killer's gun skids across the floor like a number two pencil across a desk during a college entrance exam.

"Like roses on Valentine's." The pizza man groans, as his head tilts to the fourth of the five walls that make up the studies bizarre architectural design. With his free arm the cyclist liberates the rest of his beleaguered body and without looking bolts for the firearm. He grabs hold of the pistol and whips around, stumbling in the process. The slamming of a door at the rear of the mansion gives the cyclist a slight reprieve and with it he drops to the floor. A burst of manic laughter escapes his lips, but his undue joy is cut short as he looks down at his uniform, which has gone from yellow to a dull orange.

"5,4,3,2 aaannnd 1." As the cyclist finishes counting, the tranquility of the mansion is shattered by whirring sirens cutting through the midday air.

"It is good to see that things are as predictable as ever, some would say reliability is everything, though I am not too sure what that says for you, you lifeless hunk of decaying flesh." The rider says staring at the corpse. The rider looks down at the military issued firearm and grits his teeth.

"I suppose, it says a lot actually. You partake in the deaths of others, because it gives you some sick-twisted pleasure and that makes you less of a person than every being I have ever met." The cyclist says tossing the firearm toward the bloody pool oozing its way out from underneath the assassin's body, he then grabs hold of the two red ear buds that had fallen free during his fight for survival and places them into his ears as "Deceiver of Fools" by Within Temptation plays.

este

War is Peace. Freedom is Slavery. Ignorance is Strength.
----- George Orwell

The pizza man jerks his head to the right, a latex gloved hand tries to pull it straight, while a bright white light violates his dark bloodshot eyes.
"A hospital is a bit much, isn't it? Books fell on my head." The cyclist says.
"Maybe so, but the men outside want to ask you some questions and I want to make sure you understand what is happening." The doctor replies.
"This should be edifying for the both of us." The rider quips.
"I know you feel fine, but I do not want those two suits taking advantage of you. I have heard plenty of stories about what they do to people suspected of terrorism." The doctor says switching off the ophthalmoscope.
"Why did I bother surviving?" The cyclist mutters under his breath.
"Pardon?" The doctor asks.
"If I told you, you would not understand." The rider responds.
"I understand. Are you are ready for them?" The doctor inquires.
"Even if I say no, the imbecilic script their master has regurgitated for them must be followed to the asinine letter." The pizza man says like a drunk resigned to the fact that alcohol no longer cures his miseries.
"A bit stark, but if you feel like you are ready, then..." The portly physician pauses, turns her head and shouts. "Gentlemen, he is all yours."
Before the doctor's words finish bouncing off of the drab walls, the brown door swings open and two agents of mixed ethnicities stroll through the opening with an eager intent that does not bode well for the pizza man.
"Thank you doctor." The more straight laced of the pair says.
The medical practitioner looks at the two agents dressed in off the rack suits fitting each of their painted on personalities, she then turns to the pizza man and mouths "If you need me, I will be just outside the door, love."
The stocky woman in white turns to the two agents standing at the end of

bed. She gives them a physician's smile and continues toward the exit.

"I would normally proceed with social formalities, but your wallet was void of any ID, so we thought maybe you would be kind enough to furnish us with those particular details." The agent with the flashier suit states.

The cyclist tries to sit up, however a sharp metal clang prevents him.

"Are these necessary? When was the last time you read about a pizza man who is an internationally renowned assassin? Wait I take that back, you probably have." The rider says not bothering to hide his disdain.

The prudish agent moves to the left side of the bed and says. "My partner asked a question and it would be in your best interest to answer it."

"Do you honestly even care what my name is? I bet you would be more than happy to call me the pizza man for the rest of, whatever this is. It's easier for you to remember." The rider jokes as the uptight agent snarls.

"Fine! My name is Bi Sa-Ren. Now the one on the left is a Ryan and the one on the right is a Cross. Wouldn't you agree?" The rider says mockingly.

The agents glance at each other; unheard questions fly between them until finally the flamboyant agent asks. "How do you know our names?"

"You know damn well how I know those names." The rider replies.

Ryan leans in closer to the cyclist and says "Well mister comedian, I am not a doctor, but given the facial features on that smart-alecky head of yours I would have to say you are most certainly not Chinese or even East Asian if you feel the need to play some modified version of the race card."

The rider's nostrils flare at the foul odor wafting over every syllable.

"Not Chinese? Well, I imagine you see me as whatever best defines your concept of reality, but you are going to have to take my word for it. Now are we going to continue focusing on my heritage or are we going to get to the point of this messy little farce." The pizza man responds.

A well of unbridled fury erupts from the prudish agent's dull eyes.

"We can come back to the name later." The suave agent says trying to keep their partner in check. "The more important question is what were you doing at the Japanese ambassador's residence?" Cross continues.

"You know I was delivering a pizza. I am a pizza man, but I know you have been doubting that from the moment I entered that building and secondly did you know who lived there, because I did not." The cyclist replies.

"With your intellect. There is no way you're a pizza man." Ryan says.

"You know there are things called books, right? I am sure you are familiar with these leafy structures or their synthetic counterparts. Mind you, your foray into this world hinges on a bare bones subject verb object dynamic coupled with the abuse of adverbs and adjectives." The rider retorts.

Before a set of expletives can gush out of the prudish agent's mouth, "Dumb it Down" by Lupe Fiasco blares out of Cross's phone.

"This is Cross. Really? So there is absolutely no way it could be? Ryan is not going to like that. If you say so. Got it. All right, thanks." The taller Security Service member says hanging up their phone with a slight unease.

"Please do not tell me?" Ryan asks, grimacing at the thought.

"Fraid so, footage confirms it. Our sarcastic friend arrived a couple minutes before the police." Cross turns to the rider and says. "But it doesn't answer how you knew our names, or why you were covered in blood."

"You'll let a thousand peculiarities slide but an intelligent pizza man is what sticks. Fine, I suppose it is time to Teabing anyway. I was shot at by two men, one was Northern Chinese probably Shanxi ren given the accent, I am sure you figured that out and if you did not may I suggest putting down unedifying pieces of trash that pass themselves off as literature and learning a tad bit more about the cultures of your world." The cyclist grumbles.

"Would you be able to identify the men who shot at you?" Ryan asks.

"You are better than that." The cyclist says shaking his head.

"We just want you to come to the office and skim through the info we have on file, we are not asking you to actively investigate the case or anything crazy like you see in the movies." Cross says with a warm smile.

Turning to Ryan, the cyclist says. "Would you believe such rubbish?"

"That's fine, but the cuffs stay on until we get a name." Ryan retorts.

"Did you figure out it was not my name? You know you are smarter than how the media portrays you." The cyclist says closing his eyes.

"I have heard Sandi Toksvig, I know nationality has nothing to do with the ability to speak English, so yeah I already knew." Ryan responds.

"I knew I was not going to go through all this without being sucked in. I will go, not that I have a choice, but I suppose you could care less, so long as you get what you want, no matter how incoherent said wants are." The cyclist says as the afternoon sun disappears behind a cloud.

mutluluk?

Much reading is an oppression of the mind, and extinguishes the natural candle, which is the reason of so many senseless scholars in the world.
----- William Penn

The dark clouds that had pelted the rider earlier, now outline the setting sun, as for the rider he finds himself bouncing along in a black Audi RS6. "When it Comes" by Incubus shatters the silence enveloping the compact vehicle. Cross glances at the smartphone while Ryan answers the call.

"Yes? Hold on. Hostages? Where? The Korean embassy? But we have the suspect from this morning an..., Uh-huh. Fine, we'll be there." Ryan says.

"The Korean embassy? Hostages? When?" Cross questions.

"Now. Well, thirty minutes ago to be exact." Ryan replies.

Cross whips the wheel to the right, the high-performance rubber squeals while the vehicle does a 180 degree turn. A lorry, on route to a Sainsbury's, slams on its brakes, Cross's hand drops to the gearshift like an F1 driver planning to overtake on the final stretch of the Monaco Grand Prix.

"Not to be arrogant, but we all realise the implications of the word hostage and I may be getting ahead of myself, but I assume that none of them are going anywhere anytime soon, so why was that necessary? Other than entertaining the feeble minded among us, that is." The pizza man asks.

"That was skill." Cross says revving the four litre V8 engine.

"No, that stunt would be the early onset of severe mental illness and to champion such moronic actions is to cry out for the devolution of human intelligence, but hey, that is just my opinion." The cyclist responds.

"Usually you would be correct, however with the assassination this morning, things have escalated rapidly." Ryan says over Cross's grumbling.

"Please tell me you do not believe that excuse?" The cyclist asks.

"You my pizza pushing friend need to learn to relax. The world is simple, the bad guys do bad things and we catch them." Cross pipes up.

The Audi swerves to avoid hitting an elderly man. Cross's hand shoots down to the gear shift, a grinding noise shouts out. The impatient agent forces the automobile out of the path of oncoming traffic and back into the safety the three had taken for granted only moments prior.

"I only heard a man's voice, yet somehow I find myself heading toward a hostage situation with two idiots who are far too comfortable with the events occurring around them. Please tell me you have contemplated the level of sheer stupidity that this situation reflects?" The rider asserts.

"Just think of it as your chance to be in a thriller?" Ryan responds.

The Audi lurches violently to the right and pops over an unseen curb.

"Thinking has nothing to do with thrillers, whether it is those reading them, those writing them or those inhabiting them." The rider says.

"You have some seriou..." Ryan is cut short by a fireball, that would not be out of place at a shuttle launch. Onlookers and officers alike spiral through the air, an ambulance hurtles into a building and a series of shrieks serenade the encroaching darkness with their haunting rendition of humanity.

The cars, heading in the direction of the blast, wobble. The leader of the pack swerves, the car behind it is not so agile and the two vehicles collide in a disheartening meld of metal. The Audi hops the curb to avoid the collision, but instead meets a terrified young mother and a stroller built for two. Cross panics, sending the Audi into a lamp post with the force of a meteotsunami. The engine sputters until the whine of the motor ceases. The three bodies inside the Audi lay motionless. The rider's eyes open. His blurry vision catches sight of Ryan and the glass jutting out of their throat. A gurgling emanates from the opening, which the cyclist soon realises is the agent's final breath. He turns his gaze from Ryan's corpse to Cross's. The rider places his hand onto Cross's shoulder and the want to be F-1 driver's head tumbles to the side revealing the inner workings of the agent's brain.

Several gunshots snap the rider back to the demoralising present. His woozy head moves towards the terrifying sound, his hazy vision recoils at the sight of two men in body armor exiting the flame engulfed embassy while they fire on whoever is still capable of standing. Upon seeing the unmitigated carnage being inflicted, the pizza man's eyes flash with a dull sheen as if he is but a robot responding to a lifetime of pre-programmed conditioning.

"A world where murder and mayhem are desirable outcomes is a world doomed to spend eternity repeating such actions. That is until the inevitable." The cyclist says fumbling through Cross's jacket.

The rider pulls a modified M&P9 from the confines of the shiny material. He checks the chamber, the safety, then grabs the door handle, as he steps out into the street another burst of gunfire cracks the cool air like a can of soda that has been snuck into the Opera House. The man pretending to be a thoughtless puppet of an anachronistic regime hears the voice that had saved his life echo throughout the historic edifices that line his bleak vision. The man, born in a city that at this moment seems no more than a distant memory found within a crumbling madeleine, takes a deep breath and shimmies along the stream of now vacant cars lining the street.

The rider darts passed the vehicles responsible for the demise of his handlers, then dives behind a red coupé. He presses his spine against the cold exterior while his eyes sift through the wreckage. A young mother's pitiful shriek lashes out, but is silenced by another succession of bullets. "I wonder what I will be in my next life. Hopefully, if there is any justice, blind. At least then I will not have to stare at the uncaring visage before me." The rider mutters, jumping up from behind the compact vehicle. The cyclist grips the Zytel polymer, then presses the trigger and without a question as to whether he has hit his target he lines up his next shot. The terrorist on the right tumbles, the one on the left spins around, his weapon set to unleash a barrage of bullets. The burning pyres lining the slender street gives the muzzle of the QBZ-95 a demonic gloss.

The glimmer catches the cyclist's eye, the pistol in his hand slides to the left, his fingers steady and with a mumbled prayer he pulls the trigger. The firearm releases its payload and the volley of bullets strike the masked man's shoulder. The cyclist hops over the hood of the automobile and charges at the assassin like a proud Celtic warrior in the heat of battle. The masked man, even in his prone state, raises his rifle. The rider seeing that there shall be no surrender, squeezes the trigger and two bullets tear through the assassin's skull like a honey badger through the flesh of a cobra. A turgid gasping breath ends the assassin's vain struggle at salvation. "I am done! I am sick and tired of playing this juvenile game, all these psychotic escapades and their endless reiterations. I want out of this god forsaken world. I want to be free and you are going to give it to me. I do not care if I have to have crawl over to the other side and snatch my freedom from your cold dead hands." The pizza man screams as his visceral anger explodes in a third barrage of bullets.

The cyclist stands over the cadaver repeating himself, almost as if he expects an answer, but no response shall ever come. This unwavering fact escapes the rider, as do the sirens tearing through the evening sky.

Another gunshot resounds through the fiery street, a searing pain tears through the rider's shoulder and the would-be-hero crashes to the ground. He raises his gun in retaliation, but it is kicked clear from his sweaty hand as a voice says. "You are under arrest."

"You got to be fu…" The rider tries to curse at the female agent, however a size ten shoe drives into his rib cage. The wounded cyclist, without a chance to defend himself, struggles to breathe.

In

Stupidity combined with arrogance and a huge ego will get you a long way.
----- Chris Lowe

"And welcome back to the Ten O'clock news I am Jane Edwards and we
are continuing our look at the aftermath of the terrorist attacks that rocked
London to its core only three days ago. Information has still been relatively
difficult to ascertain at this point as both Japan and South Korea are
keeping a virtual stranglehold on all information in association with the two
separate incidents, however earlier today an anonymous source informed
BBC that the weapons in both attacks were standard issue for the Chinese
military. At this time China has not released a statement in regards to the
possible allegations that this evidence presents, however both South Korea
and Japan were quite quick to cast critical remarks in regards to China's
involvement and tensions between the three countries continues to grow as
one of China's aircraft carriers was seen in Korean waters…" Edwards
stops speaking for a moment. She presses her manicured hand against her
ear piece. Her soft blue eyes light up like a C.E.O.'s during the holidays.
"I have just been informed that we have received a video of the capture of
the lone terror suspect. I must warn those with small children that this
video is quite disturbing. I would advise anyone with a weak constitution to
turn away now, or to escort out anyone who might become ill at the sight
of such material. Now I am going to send it over to Martin Bell our military
correspondent to give you a better understanding of what we are seeing."
The screen cuts to a shaky and chaotic mobile phone captured video, from
one of the stores surrounding the Korean embassy. A nasally voice
moderately less posh than Edwards's cuts in and begins commentating.
"Now I must say I have had no time to analyse this clip, as we received it
moments ago, also the sound only seems to be picking up the chatter in the
store and the song "Stupid Girls" by Pink, not the actual happenings on the
street. If you look closely you can see the two masked assailants coming

the third suspect was given before being apprehended by the Security Service suggests that he was the one that stopped the attacks and not the Security Service as first established. I am uncertain as to wha…"

A bloop is heard as the television broadcasting the news is shut off.

A liver-spotted hand snatches at a mobile phone sitting on an end table that appears to be frozen in the mid 19th century. The poorly preserved appendage brings the electronic device to a face that looks like it is capable of devouring a bucket of roofing nails without so much as a grimace. A hesitant hello makes it way through the device. The irate head of the security service holding the phone does not respond in kind, instead she lets loose a torrent of anger reserved for the most moronic of miscalculations.

"What the hell was that? If it were not bad enough that I have agents, and I use that term loosely, too stupid to keep documents in their possession. I have to deal with the fact that the evening news has just shown the whole world that we have a man who saved the lives of hundreds of people billed as a terrorist and secondly who labeled him as Ali Izz? This man is not Arabic. Did no one look at his face? He could not pass for Algerian."

The voice on the other end of the line tries to explain, however the woman who looks as if she could have served under Queen Victoria is hearing none of it and cuts the apologetic party short with. "I do not care! Tomorrow morning you will hold a press conference to quash any and all fault that we will take in this case. I want this EAST ASIAN man released and if anyone is taking the hit on this one, it is most certainly you. I do not care if you have to give him a Distinguished Service Order, I want this resolved by the time I sit down to read my morning paper. Is that understood?"

The person being derided by a woman who cares less for her agents than a Scientologist does for antidepressants responds with "Yes, ma'am."

Both parties hang up their phones and the lady, who was just treated as if she were a dog who soiled the living room carpet, stands in her living room. A man in his mid-forties stares up at the woman he calls his wife.

"The boss?" The Oxford alum asks.

"Indeed." The lady says dropping her phone onto a glass coffee table.

"I take it she saw the news." The man says with a wry smile.

"Her and everyone else who still feigns interest in this country." The black haired woman says flopping on to the autumn brown couch.

out of the building indicating that the charges were more than likely set to inflict damage upon the street more so than the Korean embassy itself, which suggests this was not a genuine hostage situation, but in fact a clever ruse to attack our law enforcement officials. The two terrorists seem to be opening fire in a rather arbitrary fashion. This tells us that the attack is obviously suicidal in nature and the two men are simply trying to register as many casualties as possible before they are gunned down by our forces. We can see gunfire and a pregnant woman being shot through the abdomen. Both men quickly look back at the embassy which I would presume is to make sure that no one is trying to escape from the building. The two assailants are beginning to move down the street at a snail's pace, they seem to be getting themselves ready for the assault by our police officials. The two men inch further down the road, they seem to turn their attentions back to the embassy, as we are all aware they left several hostages still alive. Why they are so concerned with these people at this interval is unclear. One of the assailants is hit from what looks like a precision shot, that I am quite certain came from one of our agents. However I am not certain as to wear our third assailant is at this time, but I am told that he was found next to the bodies of the two others. The second attacker seems to turn around to strike back at our forces. Here we can see he is shot in the shoulder which is standard procedure to disarm a hostile threat. A second set of shots are fired and it appears that the agents at the scene felt that immobilising the target was not an option and instead opted for ending the assault as soon as possible. OK, someone is coming into the scene now it appears to be the third suspect who is said to be Ali Izz a known associate of multiple terror organisations. It appears that Mr. Izz shoots the second suspect in the forehead and then appears to stand over the target mouthing something. Now I am not certain what is going on here, but he seems to be standing there continually mouthing the same thing over and over again."
The southern commentator goes silent while the shaky video rolls on.
"Finally after what must be at least four or five minutes we can see Mr. Izz being shot in the right shoulder and arrested by a senior member of the Security Service." The analyst's voice stops as the clip fades out.
The screen flashes back to Edwards looking quite dumbfounded.
"I am not certain what we have just witnessed, however the amount of time

The man strokes the woman's back, while she gently rubs her temples.

"So, what are you going to do then?" The man questions.

"She wants me to go on television and throw myself on the coals. At best I will be able to delay the inevitable for a day, maybe two." The Security Service agent says massaging the storm brewing in her cranium.

"Are you going to let him go?" The man asks, knowing that the woman he has dedicated the last twenty years of his life to, has no choice.

"I would rather not." The woman says pulling her hands from her head.

"Rather not?" The man asks, raising an eyebrow.

The woman tries to muster a smile that has no chance of surfacing.

"I know what it looks like and to be honest we only came up with the terrorist link to buy time." The grey eyed agent says with a pause. "Before you ask. Yes, he is a hero, but when we ran him through the system we came up with nothing, he is a ghost. No, ghost is the wrong word, because ghosts at least existed at some point. He never has and even the pizza place he supposedly works for has never heard of him." The agent says.

"So you have a suspect who is attached to an assassination as well as a terror/suicide attack and seems to be linked to them solely by his desire to be there. That is a rather scary notion." The man states.

"It is, and now I am stuck with a suspect who is intelligent, extremely capable with firearms and a natural chameleon. Yet, come tomorrow I am going to have to let him go." The agent says with a defeated sigh.

"Is there no judicial precedent you can use? If you give me a day I am sure I can convince my fellow justices to help." The man says.

The agent manages a half smile and says. "I could never ask you to do that, even if deep down I want nothing more. No, the miserable truth is, I am going to release a prisoner who we at the agency are still calling pizza man. A man who given what we have seen in the last three days could snap at least four agent's necks before we could get the chance to restrain him and the worst of it is, not only do we have to deal with this strange anomaly, there is also something far greater going on in regards to the political environment in the east."

heilig

Life is hard, and a lot of people come home tired from work. If they're gonna spend half an hour reading, they want some entertainment and a sense of achievement. So that's what I give them. That's all I'm trying to do. Is that really so wrong?
----- James Patterson

The subtle aroma of the Thames wafts through the early morning air, the Millbank entrance to Thames House heaves with a collection of bodies it is unaccustomed to. The entrance's archway looms over each of the creatures awaiting an apology they do not deserve. Their phallic appendages ready to be thrust into the face of any being they find traipsing along, in the hopes they may score what they call an exclusive. For those who do not obtain pleasure from the misery of others it is what we would deem idle gossip. In the distance a child screams and like meerkats sensing danger each member of this strange collective turns in the hope that a story may be on the horizon, however all they see is a tourist's child screaming as its pink stuffed elephant rolls onto the road. The minions of faceless conglomerates that care not for factual accuracy or journalistic ethics and integrity turn their ADHD laced attentions back to the doors that hide their prey.

Behind the marble archway is a poor excuse for a foyer. At the centre of this dreary entrance hall is a woman with black hair and greying temples. Next to her is a man whose past is as empty as a college student's fridge. The pair stands in an awkward silence that hampers even the most basic of emotions. The agent, who has to pathetically suck up to the nation she is meant to protect, glares at the strange being fidgeting beside her.

"Who do you think is going to get the blame?" The pizza man asks.

The woman born Aminta Davina Heller pulls her cold eyes from her bland beige suit and says. "I am certain that I must have misheard you."

"You are going to make some vain stab at who the culprit is, but we both know that will ring false and then if pressed you will back pedal like a politician. Now if I were to venture a guess, I might suggest the CIA, because if espionage novels have taught us anything it is that the CIA did it, that and retconning a character is no hindrance." The rider smirks.

"But what does that really matter as thought is not your strong suit. Hell you and your ilk have never even contemplated the ramifications of your actions. I do not blame you, because how can I blame someone as unaware as yourself. Even as I stand here speaking directly to you, your mind constructs an invisible barrier that prevents the truth of my words from entering your pre-programmed way of thinking." The rider continues.

The woman known as Dav to her peers sneers at, what her mother would call, a bulbous septic boil on the colon of civilized society.

"You are one smug individual, I will give you that, but I will tell you this right now. I am going to find out who you are and then there will be nothing you can do to stop me, because the public might buy that whole loser who happened to be in the wrong place at the wrong time schtick. I on the other hand know you put yourself there." Heller says through gritted teeth.

The pizza man pulls a grungy piece of paper vellum and a disposable pen from the back pocket of his jeans and leans against the wall to write.

"I know my words tend to irritate, but I assure you they are perfectly structured unlike those nescient thesaurus monkeys on your side, flipping through countless pages of unknown words, hoping this charade shall hold so that they may continue to laugh in haughty derision at those who should be considered their equals." The cyclist says with an air of obscurity that even the most prolific symbologist would not be able to decipher.

The rider folds the paper vellum into a sycee then slides the pen back. The stocky forty something scowls at the being trying to provoke her.

"True, but once these doors open they will latch on to you and not let go until they have uncovered everything, because people are happy for their villains to be mysterious, but heroes get vivisected until there is nothing left but a hollow cadaver." Heller says, placing her hand on the door handle.

"Oh my you actually think I have been put in my place, but please do remember you are nothing but an uncouth spectator." The rider responds.

Heller's lips recede allowing a smirk to adorn her unhappy visage.

"I thought someone as bright and intelligent as you would have realised that you would be the main attraction in this circus." Heller spits.

"I might not have chosen to be attached to this farce, but I will have to deal with it, although I am not sure what that means to you outside of the general confusion you are experiencing now." The rider responds.

"If you are done pontificating. We have press to meet." Heller states.

Not waiting for her cohort's response Heller pushes the door open, her ears meet the nonsensical chattering of a pack of jackals. The dew that coats the air, brushes against her cheeks as if the sky is preparing her for the blows. With each step another wave of biased questioning washes over her like a summer's rain over a drought riddled farm in Chile. Heller plants her feet in front of the reporters, takes a deep breath and prepares for the nonsense.

"I would like to thank you for coming and I promise to get straight to the point. Several days ago we apprehended an individual at the site of the Buckingham bombings. Obviously due to the nature of these attacks and the fact that the suspect was found on site, with a weapon in hand, we had no other recourse, but to apprehend him. I am aware of the fact that the suspect was considered to be Ali Izz-Al-Din a known associate of multiple terror organisations, however this information did not come from any of her majesty's services and at this time we are uncertain where these rumours originated. I would like to say the suspect has been cleared of any involvement in the bombings at this time, in addition, it is the belief of this agency that this man risked his life in order to save the lives of others and this act is worthy of your admiration, further more we are proud to state that he will be honoured at a later date for his courage. Now I have time for two questions and please do remember that this investigation is ongoing, so keep your questions focused on the man and his actions." Heller says.

"Is this apology based on the fact that MI5 was caught holding a man who had nothing to do with the terror attacks? And if so does this not shine a negative light on an organisation with an all ready poor public image?" A balding middle-aged man, who thinks a custard yellow turtleneck and a light grey tweed jacket is fashionable, asks with a condescending tone. Heller remains as calm as one would expect, however in the recesses of her mind a juvenile voice shouts *You spent all bloody morning coming up with that! A blind incontinent primate could walk by that poorly laid minefield.*

"The reason this apology is being delivered in this manner is due to the hype surrounding a certain video, had it not been for this video we would have conducted this apology in private and of course in a much more dignified manner as for the negative light comment, that is opinion rather than fact." Heller's words are as bland as plain, over-cooked white rice. Heller waves her hand across the feral crowd until it lands upon a bored woman whose youthful vigour suggests that inside she believes that celebrity meltdowns are more important news stories than this.

"We were told we would be able to speak with the pizza man? I'm curious as to when he'll be available for questioning?" The young reporter asks. Heller turns to face the rider. She anticipates seeing the infuriating being she is being forced to release, however only a gentle breeze, toying with the fabric of time and space, remains. Heller, knowing that she has to pretend that the entire spectacle is going to plan, turns to the flippant reporter and says. "Like any hero he does not want to become a spectacle, he feels that what he did is something that anyone else given the situation, would have done and he would appreciate if the media would respect his wishes and I for one am not going to deny a man's request to savour his privacy, because if we as a nation cannot respect an individual's right to privacy then surely we have allowed ourselves to become a nanny state and I know no one in the media would want that. Now I am sorry I must leave as we do still have an investigation ongoing and there are many things to be done." Without giving the frothing reporters a second glance Heller turns her back on them. The infuriated agent moves quickly as the remnants of unanswered questions bounce off her. She grabs the half circle in the middle of the door and swings it open expecting to see the rider, but her vision is not greeted with her expectations. The agent's lips quiver, a curse word, that would cause her conservative grandmother to faint, dances on her vocal chords. Heller's first instinct is to find the pizza man, however her mind tells her. *There is no point. He is weaving in and out of the clueless masses, like an icy breeze through the frigid branches of a Siberian forest, at this moment.* Min, as she is loving referred to by her husband, stares at the space where the rider stood, her mind calculating everything that has occurred. A sudden flash lights her eyes, her hand reaches into her pocket. Her fingers feel for the object she knows is there. She pulls the sycee free and unfolds it.

How could I vanish into thin air? You know the answer, all you have to do is wake up and see the truth. The black ink reads.

ACT II

An Expositional Engagement

raamatud

Universal education is the most corroding and disintegrating poison that
liberalism has ever invented for its own destruction.
----- Adolf Hitler

"I am standing in front of Lancaster house where the cold war styled stand-
off between three of the most powerful nations in the world will come to
ahead at what is hopefully the last of the four nation talks. As has been
custom since the beginning of these discussions five years ago, the talks are
being held once more in London as Britain being the odd one out in this
grouping feels the need to have it on neutral soil. This weekend will also
mark the sixth anniversary of the Buckingham bombings. A coincidence, I
think not. In this reporter's honest opinion these discussions will do nothing
more than fuel the growing aggression that most of the world is feeling
towards China's new status as the economic superpower. We have been led
to believe the talks will focus more on the disputed maritime territories of
each nation, as well as China's dismissal of any responsibilities in regards
to the Buckingham bombings even after it was proven that the three
deceased terrorists were still considered active members of the Chinese
military at the time of the attacks. How will this all play out? Given what
we have seen from the last few times these three were at the negotiation
table. We can expect China not to concede anything and given what the
Chinese delegate articulated during the last round of negotiations in regards
to Japan getting what they deserve, I feel that we will see these rivalries
continue to spread without any nation considering what is best for their
people and the development of the world as it continues to rebuild from the
deadly Ondatra virus that wiped out the entire population of the Americ…"
"Stop right there." A slimmer version of Agent Heller shouts.
One of Heller's overworked subordinates tries to follow her boss's
overzealous directions, however the sleep deprived technician pauses the
news feed several frames too late. The small screen freezes on the camera

panning across the warm honey coloured walls of Lancaster House, the former home of the London Museum, while several East Asian tourists, in novelty t-shirts, take false memories for their digital scrapbooks.

"Rewind until you see the yellow polo shirt." Heller almost shouts.

The video clip skips backwards, at the pace of a sea anemone in heat, until the broad face of the pizza man appears in the corner of the grainy feed.

"Focus on the lower right quadrant and enhance the picture." Heller says.

The screen distorts as the technician tries to give Heller what she wants.

"Is that the best you can do? What is the point of spending millions of pounds if all we can produce is no better than a photofit drawn by Paul Klee." Heller says showing that digital technology is not her forte.

"We can use spatial anti-aliasing, but it is not going to clean up the picture to the extent you desire, but it should be at least semi-recognisable, aside from that there is not much else I can do, though I suppose if you give me some time I can filter the image through a graphic redistribution agent and it should be able to recompile the picture." The technician says forgetting that technical knowledge is something that most agency heads are lacking.

"I do not care what it is called, or what it does, so long as we get a clearer picture of that man. That is all that matters." The agency head states.

The baggy eyed technician grumbles under her ramen noodle scented breath, while she tries to achieve Heller's nearly impossible request.

With each click of the out-of-date keyboard, the rugged facial features of the man in the yellow polo shirt becomes a distorted mess of pixels.

"It is the pizza man." Heller says with renewed vigour.

The technician turns her head to the side and stares at her superior.

"If you want me to order some pizza, I suppose I could, but I don..."

"The man in the yellow polo shirt is the pizza man." Heller snarls.

"O...K.?" The technician responds with a raised eyebrow and pursed lips.

"Send copies of that image out to every police station in Greater New Britain as well as every agency, with a request to pick him up on sight and a warning to proceed with caution." Heller says with a slight twitch.

"Sure thing, ma'am." The technician says reconfiguring the picture.

Heller scrutinises the blurry image. The cogs in her mind turn and thoughts of the pizza man's plans take hold of her brain. Heller gives the screen one last look then heads for the oak door on the other side of the room.

The door swings open and Heller steps out into the basement's dimly lit corridor, her black smart phone already pressed against her ear. "Cummings. Heller here. I have the com techs working on reconfiguring a distorted image of a terror suspect. I need you to go to the archives and pull file 26491-HCN, it is a red file. I want you and the team briefed on the man in the dossier before I get to you. Uh-huh. I will be there in an hour. I do not care what you have on your plate. This is top priority, as it may be linked to a terror plot directed at the four party talks this weekend. Got it? Good. See you soon." Heller says dropping her phone into her pocket. Heller reaches the elevator doors then presses the button marked up and recoils in doubtful anticipation. The faltering light above the lustreless metal door flashes and an effeminate ding echoes through the drab walls of the military bunker. The silver box slides its toothless maw open revealing a russet coloured room and mirrors stained with extramarital obsessions. Heller steps inside the half room/half vessel and mutters "I have got you." as she slaps the metallic button for the third floor. A sudden pain bounces off the walls of Heller's skull and lands in her right eye. She squints and as she does the face hidden amongst the lustful fingerprint forest morphs into the rider's. The chimerical visage smiles and says. "Insanity? Or is it sanity bleeding into fantasy? You have to figure out which is which. Sad, isn't?" As the last of these non-existent expressions splash across Heller's dumbfounded face, the strange optical illusion morphs back, the disorientated agent's blood shot eyes blink *as if reality is set to return once the pain in her mind vanishes*. A blurry residue distorts her perception for another moment, but she does not get a second more to think about the strange occurrence that has just transpired inside the metal womb as the doors to this silver coffin open.

ɔnɩɓɯդրηɩɯ

I've given up reading books. I find it takes my mind off myself.
----- Oscar Levant

The midday warbles of an upscale cafe ring out, patrons clamouring for
overpriced drinks and snacks. Heller's gaze drifts over lime green armchairs
and cosmic latte settees situated near nouveau chic tables and in those
hideous pieces of form-cum-fad fashion sit the silver spoon collective who
are wasting their exorbitant amount of free time on formulaic novels that
history has already forgot, but these dilettantes of nothingness hold no
interest for the aged agent. Her only concern is a small table at the back
with a pair of worn Doc Martens and a light green bag-for-life underneath it.
Without saying a word Heller sits down at the cluttered table, across from
her sits Washington Irving's most famous character brought to life.
"Mr. Jefferies, I would presume?" Heller says with a dry mouth.
"You are late. One would hope things of this nature would be deemed more
important than a careless encounter in a High Street coffee shop." Jefferies
says bringing his steel blue eyes up to meet Heller's grey pools of loathing.
Heller places her arthritic hands on the sticky table, a short but pronounced
click reverberates as something plastic makes it presence known.
"I suppose it is to be expected of people such as yourself. Your kind if I may
say so, do not even have the proper level of refinement to offer a suitable
greeting before making yourself at home like a distended sow in a sty full of
swill. No, your kind, see the world as owing you some sort of debt." The
grey haired man posing as one Mister Barrington Jefferies the third says.
"I am sorry, I thought snide handshakes and pats on the back had slid out of
style along with the bobby sock." Heller says extending her right hand out.
Jefferies glances at Heller's slow extension and reciprocates in kind.
"Courtesy costs nothing. Mind you I have come to expect the worst from
you people and even in that expectation I have overestimated those that
dream of being emperors." Jefferies says sliding his wrinkled hand back.

"That is one way of looking at things." Heller says, crossing her legs.

"There are two ways of looking at things. Both of which lead us to delusions that are better left buried. If not, they become the inspiration for fanatical madmen." Jefferies says, tucking the flash drive into his bag-for-life.

"That is an interesting world view you are sporting, but I feel that there can only be one genuine outcome no matter how many ways of looking at something there is and in that outcome we see the truth for what it is." Heller says fishing her wallet out of her inside jacket pocket.

"I would love to continue this extraneous conversation with you, however I am quite certain there is a pampas in need of my direct supervision, so I will say good day and offer you my most humble apologies." Jeffries's crotchety tone is contradicted by the spry nature in which he stands up.

"I would say, I hope you enjoy yourself, but I am unsure whether that is even possible anymore." Heller says rifling through the bills in her wallet.

"I shall try, if for no other reason than the joy of spiting you and throwing that arrogance back in your face. However it may take me a day or two to do just that, so please hold your breath." Jefferies says lifting up the bag.

Heller, flagging down a barista, says. "I am certain, I could think of at least fifty thousand reasons why putting a rush on it is a necessity."

"Even with so many reasons one cannot always obtain what they are after any sooner. They must make do with what they get." Jefferies responds.

"I suppose not, just thought I would put it out there. Anyway, I am sorry to keep you. You have yourself a wonderful day." Heller's words slide off her forked tongue with such lingual dexterity that her boarding school teachers would smile if they were still capable of feeling human emotions.

The older gentleman's shoes click against the California Gold Slate tile that lines every inch of the coffee shop, while his hand escorts out a bag that contains a government file pertaining to a man who vanished from the face of the earth five years ago. A being incapable of existing, yet bafflingly does, a creature so heinous that his presence is a threat to the world in which he lives. Jefferies as he prefers to be called on this day is now tasked with trying to discover what if anything the pizza man has to do with the upcoming four party talks.

разведка

I would rather entertain and hope the people learned something than educate people and hope they were entertained.
----- Walt Disney

The eyes of the political world are locked on London, because in twenty-four hours, four of the world economic powers will meet, yet the pulse of the city does not register this palpitation. Off-white clouds still crowd the sky, chilly weather still gnaws the bones and a cluster of tourists still surround Guy Fawkes's greatest failure, their feet clogging the roadways causing chauffeurs and cabbies to grumble about the foreigners that plague their once beautiful city. All the while the patrons in the backseat watch glasses empty or meters rise. For Heller it is the latter that should concern her, but the bouquet sitting on the lap of the man known as Jefferies, is her only concern. Heller's bureaucratic masters desire what is hidden in the folds of the lush petals, while Heller wants a single name. The name of a being that has been dancing in her mind, like a Lynchian inspired ballerina.
"Cutting it a tad close, Benedict?" Heller says raising her eyes.
"Her birthday is not until tomorrow and I wanted to make sure they were as fresh as possible." Jefferies says handing over the purple and pink medley.
"They look exquisite. I am certain she will adore them." Heller responds.
"That is kind of you to say but, she was looking for something spectacular, these are no more than a pale imitation." Jefferies responds.
"So long as they were on the list. I am certain that she will take to them like a child to sugar." Heller says channelling a daytime talk show host.
"Sadly, they were not. Oh and please do apologise about my missing dinner. I am completely swamped with work and I have to take the daughter to the British museum." Jefferies says getting ready to vacate the vehicle.
"One's children must always come first." Heller replies.
"Excuse me driver, if you could be so kind as to please pull the vehicle over that would be greatly appreciated." Jefferies says far too politely.

"You are getting out here?" Heller asks.

"Indeed. I have to pop over to the CPA for a moment and deal with some strange irregularities. You know how it is." Jefferies responds.

"But of course and please do send me the cleaning bill for that suit. Again I have to apologise for the clumsiness of my assistant." Heller says.

"Don't mention it. Have yourself a wonderful evening and do give the old gal my best wishes." Jefferies says stepping out of the black cab.

"I shall and send my warmest regards to the wife." Heller responds.

The mentally preoccupied agent watches through the fingerprint infested window as Jefferies disappears into the crowd like an albino polar bear into the Arctic tundra. Her gaze drifts from the shapes outside to the bouquet on her lap. Her hand toys with the pink fabric while her heart shouts *tear it open, right now*. Screeching brakes awake Heller from her inner musings.

"How much do I owe you?" Heller says reaching into her pocket.

"That'll be twenty quid, ma'am." The cabbie responds.

Heller steps out into the cool air, the bitter wind nips at her dry skin. The bouquet ascends to the sky absconding with the secrets hidden within its delicate folds. Heller snatches at the multi-coloured camouflage, but the tulips and lilacs crash into the ground. Her body freezes at the sight of a pair of masculine hands grabbing hold of the bouquet of flowers.

"Leave them alone." Heller shouts at the top of her lungs.

The arms pull back, Heller bends down to take hold of her scented prize. She reaches inside the bouquet and with a sigh of relief she feels the hard plastic as well as a piece of thin cardboard. Heller pulls both free, revealing the jet-black ink on the embossed card. **Wondering why I am here, or have you lost the plot entirely? Not that you would ever admit it.** Heller's head snaps up and her eyes feverishly search for the pizza man, but as quick as his sleight of hand had been, his disappearing act had been just that much quicker.

mint

I am not a fan of books. I would never want a book's autograph.
I am a proud non-reader of books.
----- Kanye West

A tinge of orange flesh lies on a bed of white, nestled next to an onyx sea. A pair of round chopsticks descends on a slab of succulent saki salmon, but their efforts are in vain. The miniature fork off to the side is of no comfort to the man behind the sticks, for in his world face stands above all else. The aged fingers of the justice of the peace regroup and clench the metal prongs tighter. He squeezes them around the fish and lifts it off the avocado coloured slate. His eyes glance at the chômiryô sara filled with soy sauce, but pride pushes away any possible attempts at adding the black concoction to the buttery texture of the salmon. Suddenly the phone in his breast pocket vibrates. The unexpected jolt of life sends the sashimi spiralling downward.
"Bloody hell." The justice says pulling his phone free.
"James?" The voice on the other end of the line asks.
"Min?" James utters grabbing the stray sashimi with his serviette.
"Are you free to talk at the moment?" Heller questions.
James's gaze moves across the minimalist interior of the upscale sushi restaurant to the oak archway that highlights the nouveau kenchiku door.
"I am eating." He replies while his green eyes move to a gigolo, his sugar mama paying the bill and the young waitress standing at the register.
"So is that a yes or no?" Heller asks.
"I thought we agreed not to speak until after the divorce." James says.
"I wanted to make sure you are all right." Heller responds.
"And…" James replies.
"I just wanted you to be careful this weekend. In fact it might be better if you went to see Jane and Felix until Monday, maybe Tuesday." Heller says.
"Why, pray tell? Are Chinese greengrocers going to sneak into my apartment and choke me to death with ramen or is it going to be a Russian

borscht dealers and a rotten potato?" James says rolling his eyes.

"James, stop being so childish about this." Heller says with authority.

"I am on the wrong side of fifty, Min. Is it necessary to play the child card? Or has this obsession of yours seeped so far into your brain that you are no longer able to see the funny side of anything." James replies.

"I know de... James. It is stressful, what with the four party talks and not to let the cat out of the bag, but we have received intelligence in regards to an attempt this weekend and I would feel much better if you were out of the city. " Heller says uncharacteristically following her heart.

"Thank you for being so candid and I suppose it has been far too long since I last saw Jane and Felix. Mind you, I am certain it has been absolutely eons since you last saw them. At least since the baby was born." James says as his eyes catch sight of a delivery man exiting the kitchen.

"I would love to see them. Hopefully after this, with the field behind me and maybe..." Heller says hoping James will fill in the blanks.

"Maybe then you will stop and enjoy life, maybe some fine dining. Mind you the staff at this restaurant are philistines. They serve up exquisite sushi, yet they are in the back eating greasy pizza." James scoffs.

"Pizza? What colour is the uniform?" Heller questions her ex.

"It is light yellow." James says not connecting the dots.

"James, get out of there this instant. It's him." Heller blurts out.

"Min, it was five years ago, he was jus..." The blast the justice never heard bounces off the walls of a lavatory. Heller's hand drops to her side and the phone it held falls to the floor. Her body lurches forward, she reaches for the tap but the sight of a yellow polo shirt in the mirror stops her.

"Of all the places to blow up, why that one? Poor hygiene? An inside job, perhaps? Or maybe it was so that you would feel manipulated into caring. Too bad you are incapable of such an emotion." The cyclist states.

Heller whips her head around, but there is no one there, only Urami Bushi by Meiko Kaji ringing out from her phone.

একটি

Facts are meaningless.
You can use facts to prove anything that's even remotely true!
----- Homer J. Simpson

A crisp wind pushes a plastic piece of disposable culture across the brickwork of Byng Place. Its quivering form pirouettes in front of the Darwin Building then trots by the Grant Museum until it hovers over Gower Street like a sleep deprived parent over the cradle of a newborn child.
The inanimate vessel spirals toward the decaying foliage passing as a bus shelter. It swoops and dives along the ever changing air currents until its frail form is snatched out of the disapproving air by a prepubescent hand.
"Drop that this instant, Tarquin." A posh sounding woman commands. Within seconds the plastic container drops to the ground and the young boy, who resembles a porcelain doll more so than a seven year old, looks up at his overbearing mother with watery eyes that say "Sorry, please do not strike me again." The pleading message in his gaze is not received by this supposed parental figure. Her gloved hand strikes with the speed of a cobra and the juvenile's effeminate shoulder plays the part of the hapless mouse. The synthetic container, unaware of the torment it is has wrought, takes off into the docile grey atmosphere, but this sudden resurgence is short lived as it crashes into the face of a clean shaven man wearing a yellow polo shirt. The enigmatic being known only as the pizza man searches for a rubbish bin to place the holey bag in, however no such container crosses his path and with a sense of ecology he stuffs the piece of plastic into his back pocket. The saboteur then moves along the pavement through the masses of urban camouflage. His disenchanted gaze falls upon an out of place pub. "The Green Heron? Well, that is subtle. Could have been worse, though. it could have been bastardized Italian." The pizza man remarks to himself. The nameless creature, escorting a pale carrier bag with a gaudy logo, crosses the patched pavement next to University College Hospital.

Outside the back entrance a patient sneaks a drag off a cancerous stick she promised her family she had quit. Several St. John Ambulance drivers chuckle in the face of the overwhelming depression looming over each of their skulls like debt over a Central African nation, but on this day no vice, nor jape will save those that inhabit this glass mausoleum. The doctors and nurses trying desperately to pre-empt death's inevitable victory, struggle in vain for death has come to call and not even the newly donated painting of Avalokiteshvara can save them from the carnage that shall soon take place.

ACT III

Ne Plus Ultra

זִיבַד.

Ideas are more powerful than guns.
We would not let our enemies have guns,
why should we let them have ideas.
----- Joseph Stalin

A jet-black Audi slinks by the British Library heading west on Euston road, the compact motor vehicle tries its best to manoeuvre around the honking automobiles alongside it, but much to the chagrin of the driver, the idiotic motorists surrounding her have no concept of an emergency or of their own abysmal driving skills. The motorist catches sight of an opening. Her foot slams down on the accelerator, the owner of the blue Citroen she cuts off lays on their horn. The Audi bursts through the T-junction. A cyclist in a red shell suit swerves out of the way and crashes into the side of a ghoulish bus. The agitated driver of the black RS6 crosses over the dotted line and into what should be a flurry of oncoming traffic, but the road before her is as clear as the waters off Langkawi. The buildings and those that still feel the need to obey the stringent laws of the road are but a blur to the driver, her cold eyes focus on the blockade several blocks ahead and as the police vehicles and panic stricken masses become a part of the foreground the driver decelerates and pulls up to a scene of carnage that western society has deemed acceptable so long as it is found in the Middle East, however this obsidian shard of a vehicle is not pulling up to an open air market in the less desirable parts of Baghdad, but, to a hospital in the centre of London.
 The car door opens and Heller joins the fray in front of the hospital turned hospice. "Chief!" Shouts a feminine voice through the crowded masses. The micromanaging head of operations turns toward the hurried cry.
"You have to see this." A blonde haired agent in her thirties shouts.
The plump blonde rushes to inform her superior of the grave atrocities hidden beneath the debris, the black container in her chubby hands bounces along like a loose ponytail in the latter stages of a gruelling triathlon.

"What is it, Lebel?" Heller asks rubbing her temples.

"A list of their demands. Well actually, I should say demand, as in singular." Lebel says setting the dark coloured case upon the hot hood of the Audi. Lebel unsnaps the two gold plated locks and lifts the lid revealing a series of lacquered bamboo slips bound together by a coarse black thread.

"You have had it checked?" Heller asks eyeing the paramedics.

"The girls in the bomb squad said it was clean and there are no traces of foreign compounds on the bamboo slips." Lebel replies.

"Where did they find it?" Heller asks as her gaze returns to the case.

"At the moment, we believe it was hidden inside a pizza carrier, but to be honest this is more speculation than anything." Lebel responds.

"Given the evidence we have gathered from the previous site that is a fair summation to make." Heller states picking up the bamboo slips.

"They have been planning this for a long time, haven't they?" Lebel asks.

"Anyone who is willing to carve their demands with technology that was abandoned centuries ago, is someone who is highly ideological and a person like that has nothing but time to kill." Heller says unfolding the slips. "Do we have anyone on site that reads Chinese or do we have to waste another hour searching for a bloody translator?" Heller continues.

"Actually, I can speak Cantonese and Mandarin." Lebel responds.

Heller raises her eyebrows at Lebel's remark forcing the heavyset woman to say. "My dad was stationed in and around Hong Kong for several decades."

"Then these are all yours." Heller says handing the slips over to Lebel.

"We the ancestors of Liu Bang demand that all East Asian nations fall back into line and rejoin the only true East Asian kingdom. We demand that all foreign devils cease their dealings with East Asian nations until they are all once more a part of our glorious dynasty. Failure to comply will result in attacks on every major city that harbours these dangerous separatists and to prove our intentions, bombs have been placed in Acton as well as New Malden. If your pathetic government does not broadcast our demands very soon, then more shall die." With a look of confusion Lebel finishes.

"But there are no demands, aside from the one requesting that we broadcast their demands. Am I missing something or...?" Lebel asks.

"The demands were in the case we found in South Kensington." Heller says as Lebel sets the bamboo slips back into the charcoal case.

"I know the official stance is that we do not negotiate, but what is the protocol for something of this magnitude?" Lebel questions.

"First off we get the locals to shut this place down. Secondly, I want all hospitals in the area put on high alert. Aside from that we have to take them at their word, so I want extra units stationed in both of the areas mentioned and on top of that I want all businesses private or public closed and a curfew put in place. I want these streets empty and for the love of all that is holy. I want all the delegates here for the four party talks tucked away somewhere safe." Heller says like a dictator in the midst of a coup d'etat.

"But why would they bomb a sushi restaurant and a teaching hospital near Euston Square?" Lebel asks even though she knows the answer.

"They are looking to divide and conquer. We now have two crimes scenes that are at least an hour or more away from the others, our resources are stretched to the breaking point, thus allowing him and whoever else to escape scot-free, unlike last time." Heller says shaking her head.

"But we had the bastard last time." Lebel says showing her age.

"That is the greatest trick of all, how do you walk into places and not be suspected as a terrorist in the midst of a series of high-profile bombings? The answer to that is quite simple, be caught on video and become immortalized as a hero." Heller says as she slams the lid of the case.

"I feel like I should be impressed." Lebel says raising an eyebrow.

Heller goes to respond, but Meiko Kaji cuts through the air.

"This is Heller. On camera? When? Thirty minutes ago. Got it. He is to be detained on sight, shoot to kill only if left with no other recourse and send a copy of those images to my phone now. Lebel will be calling in with an update on movements. O.K., bye." Heller says hanging up her phone.

"We have caught a break here. We have CCTV footage of the pizza man leaving the hospital an hour ago." Heller states with renewed vigour.

"Excellent, but he could be halfway to either site." Lebel says.

"Or he is nearby. That is why you are going to do as I said and I am going to search for him." Heller states, fishing her keys out of her pocket.

"I mean no offence by this chief, but there is no way you are going to be able to find him by yourself, even if he is still somehow in the local vicinity, because by now he will have changed his clothes and vanished." Lebel says forgetting that such candour ruins careers.

"No, this is a game to him and that uniform is a way to prove that he is a genius. He wants to show us that he can pull this off even though his uniform makes him stand out like an abstentious man in a monastery." Heller says with a zealot's certainty that the facts do not support.

"But Ma'am I do no…" Lebel tries to speak her mind, but is cut-off.

"Stop thinking and grab that case." Heller says opening her car door.

The Audi's engine comes to life and within another second its wheels are spinning and the compact car becomes a memory, leaving the younger agent clutching the black case, unsure of what to do about the deadline they have been given.

Яагаад?

How well he's read, to reason against reading!
----- William Shakespeare

The pillars of curling smoke and ash clouds choking downtown London are
for the citizens of New Malden a foreign concept like cuneiform. For at this
moment the sun highlights this suburban escape and idle creatures walk
from block to block. Amongst these faces one can see a heavy Korean
influence, but one could not mistake this part of the world for Seoul or even
the rustic countryside of Gangwon-do, though several of the locals might
argue the case. In reality New Malden appears to resemble any town located
behind the walls of Greater New Britain save for the occasional Hangul.
Just off the intersection of Penrith and Kensington, a Korean couple in the
spring of their romance sit at a wooden picnic table. The white canopy
above deflects the rare London sunshine from their youthful flesh.
With one final click of the button the young woman, or girl as she would
prefer, ceases her photographical endeavours. She places the cracked
Samsung down on the picnic table. With a bat of heavily mascaraed
eyelashes she notices the seconds roll over, leaving a four followed by a
succession of zeros, she brings her naïve brown eyes up to meet the
ravenous face of her pudgy lover, she gazes past the rotund features into
thoughts of a future that has yet to be written, but these idyllic thoughts
vanish as the world around her explodes into one of smoke and charred
rubble. Her startled brain tries to cope with the sudden distortion, however
her mind's ability to slow down reality only serves to horrify her psyche
with tales of excruciating torture and death in its most infantile form.
The former miss Yi watches with hypnotic assuredness as her lover's skull
is torn asunder by a piece of the off-white beam meant to stabilise the
awning. The searing heat of the blast singes her ghostly flesh, stealing the
media centric beauty she has spent far too many hours trying to perfect. Her
ears ring for but a second and then the concept of sound is stolen from her

and if she was still capable of hearing the world around her, she might have taken note of a second blast behind her, but this world is no longer hers to comprehend and all that she was, has been blotted out in a act of calculated fear. All those dreams, hopes and fantasies, that she had cradled, are but false memories of a life that would never be lived, nor known of.

A passing Land Rover is the next in a long line of victims. The oversized vehicle veers off its original path and the former RAF member inside, struggles with her uncooperative steering wheel, while her trusty Irish wolfhound howls in the back. The fight between woman and machine lasts for but a mere moment. The winner on this day? A hunk of metal, which has chosen the front window of a brick house to deposit its former owner.

Those lucky enough not to be a part of the events that would later be broadcast over national television, in grainy CCTV footage, watch on with muted shock. Most of the onlookers stand as if someone has replaced their legs with stone pillars, yet a single woman of Caribbean descent finds the courage to run in the direction of the charred remains of civilisation. Without an air of concern for her own well-being she runs inside the burning building that once sported a large green sign. The dark-skinned woman as brave as she is, would not make it back out, save for in a darkened fortress of eternal silence masquerading as a coroner's black bag and the news as well as her relatives would never know how courageous she truly was.

The smoke from the fires building inside these former business rises up to the pristine blanket of blue and white that hovers over the mourning masses and brave officers. The sky's serene vestige allows the world to forget that somewhere out there in amongst the winding side streets of Central London, a lone figure, that has nothing in their heart save for hate, lurks. This diabolical fiend stalks the streets hidden within his bright yellow camouflage and as his feet collide with the pavement a vile chortle escapes the venomous cesspool he calls his mouth.

Sepse

The primary task of a useful teacher is to teach
his students to recognize 'inconvenient' facts -
I mean facts that are inconvenient for their party opinions.
----- Max Weber

The smouldering pyres of devastation that coat the skyline of London push
even the bravest residents of this metropolis indoors. Those left out on this
invisible battlefield are those who have sworn to uphold the law, those who
risk their lives battling infernos and those who uphold the Hippocratic Oath.
Each member of this fraternity of salvation fights the escalating insanity
that consumes the city, even when the news of the blast in Acton dashes all
hope. With this gnawing anxiety dwelling deep within their souls, each
member of this collective fights for a city that mocks them and more often
than not hinders their progress. Today, however there are no hindrances, as
their vehicles are the only things coasting along the forsaken city streets.
In between the sirens and the risks, creeps an Audi. The mother of one
within scans each alleyway for the obtuse insignia she is looking for. A sign
that she cannot convince herself exists, yet cannot bring herself to stop
searching for. A quick case of ringxiety sends Heller's eyes darting to her
phone. They glare at the GPS map for a moment. Waiting for that glowing
screen to flash and a voice on the other end to tell her that a bomb has gone
off and at this point giving in to the terrorist's demands is the only way, but
the screen does no more than adjust as she turns left on to Euston Rd.
An opaque shaft of light shoots across the stressed agent's peripheral vision.
She squeezes her eyelids tight hoping to combat the first stage of a blinding
migraine, a migraine that finds its home in a pulsating blob of black
malignant cells hidden deep within the walls of her aging brain.
"Argh, Not bloody now. You can kill me when I am done with this case and
not a moment sooner." Heller grumbles to herself, her left hand reaches into
the driver's console in search of her doctor prescribed pain medication. Her

gaze drifts from the empty road. She catches sight of the brown bottle and pulls it from its hiding place, but as it comes into view Heller realises that there is not a pill left within the cinnamon casing's confines.

"God damn it, Min." Heller says aloud but in her head the sentence carries on. *You have to pull yourself together. You are letting the world as you know it crumble around you. All because of some psychopath in a yellow polo shirt. You are sm…* Heller's internal monologue is interrupted by a figure in a yellow polo shirt, with a smile one would relish slapping, standing in the centre of the street. Heller's instincts take over and her hand jerks the wheel. Heller's primal actions leave her vehicle sitting in the middle of oncoming traffic and if this had been any normal day, she would now be waiting for the paramedics to save her life. Instead, Heller slams the vehicle into park and steps out on to the desolate street. She searches for the man that had been there only moments prior, but her brain reminds her there was never a man, yellow shirted or otherwise, just a cancerous delusion brought into 3D. Heller shakes her aching skull in disgust at her failing eyesight, when all of a sudden another yellow reflection appears in the corner of her eye. *James was right. You are letting this pizza man notion get out of control. You are seeing yellow everywhere. Just take a damn look at it, so that you can quench your curiosity and then let's actually try to catch the terrorist instead of looking for this delusional fairy tale brought to life. Please?* Heller follows her own sound advice and turns the marching band passing as her cranium toward the hallucination, however unlike her previous manifestations there is no yellow polo shirt mocking her, no strange figure with an odd glint in its chaotic brown eyes. There is no convoluted exposition of superiority. There is only a canary yellow BMX chained to a railing in front of the British Library.

Ваш

Textbooks are Soviet propaganda.

----- Jerry Falwell

A finger turns the fragile pages of a tome written in the ninth century. It moves along the intricate hanzi extracting the knowledge held within these radiant strokes via osmosis. The elaborate grouping of radicals unfolds a tale of a lost slipper and a king's endless search for a fair maiden. The youthful digit glides to the bottom of the page then rises in search of the next tale. The sheets turn into a blur as the reader searches for something in particular, a tale involving the legendary Wu Gang and a waxing moon. "People are being massacred and you are here in the British Library having a relaxing read." Heller says yanking the text out of her target's hands. "This is a conundrum. It should be closed, right? I mean it is only logical, yet here I am. If I told you it involved Chekhov's gun would that put you at ease? I suppose not. You still rely on the whims and cues of those who mock humanity with their very existence." The rider responds. "What will it take to stop this?" Heller says glancing at the book. "The question on everyone's mind, but I am certain that you want this mystery to continue, that way you get to continue to pretend that you are more than a vacuous cog in a capitalistic dystopia." The cyclist says. The recent widow fires the Chinese relic into a bookshelf that houses a trillion forgotten fantasies. The tumbling piece of ancient literature crashes to the ground, at the same time Heller swings her left arm at the rider's obnoxious skull, but the snake like pizza man slithers free. "What is with you people and your desire for violence. You spend your entire lives deploring such acts, yet deep within the cavernous pits of your jet-black hearts sits an insatiable lust for brutality against the humanity you champion. How macabre you are." The pizza man says turning to run. "Not this time. I'm not going to let you destroy this world or all the innocent people in it." Heller says shaking off her mistake.

Heller's arthritic knees pop as she tries to keep up with her younger counterpart. Her mind wavers between the now and an agonising tempest of destructive illusions and Shakespearean allegories. Somewhere between these states Heller loses herself and her eyes miss the copy of Fyodor Dostoyevsky's "The Idiot". Heller stumbles and a trickle of blood makes its way down her lip. Her head snaps back in the direction of the rider, only to see that the yellow phantom she was chasing has vanished yet again.

"No. Not again." Heller shouts at the tranquil air surrounding her.

Heller pushes her body harder than it has been pushed in the last decade. A painful jab strikes her right temple as her head swivels to check every bookcase she passes, her brow tenses trying to fight off the pain, but with each desperate glance the darkening thunder clouds, hidden behind her eyes, shoot forth another torturous bolt. Her mind screams of failure and acceptable defeat. That is until she happens upon an out of place fire exit. Heller crashes through the door causing the alarm to tear at her psyche. Between the shrieking blasts violating her ears and the electric circus dancing along her nerve endings Heller questions *Why didn't the siren sound. Did he go this way or* the sound of footsteps below sets Heller at ease and her legs back at full stride. Heller rounds the corner and through the audio distortion surrounding her, she hears the sound of a door open, an impulse that would be more commonly found in an adolescent takes over and the aging service member jumps down the remaining flight of steps. As her feet touch the ground instincts that have lay dormant since her days in the field kick into action, her body slams into the wall allowing her frame to alleviate the excess pressure being applied to her ankles. With one swift push her body moves off the grimy ill coloured wall and toward a red door that she hopes hides the escaping form of the pizza man and not another dose of unreality.

지도자

When I read about the evils of drinking, I gave up reading.
----- Henny Youngman

Heller's eyes reopen to the sound of screeching tires and the sight of the pizza man rolling off the side of a late twentieth century Volvo. *Finally, he screwed up.* Heller thinks, freeing her Walther P99 from its holster.
"Sir, I am going to need you to stay in your vehicle. The man you just struck is a terrorist and I am an MI-5 agent." Heller shouts at the driver.
"He is starting to move." The driver's mouth motions.
The driver's impotent words stir a panic in Heller's convulsing brain, but this panic is silenced by the man behind the wheel bringing a .22 calibre pistol into view. The woman in the suit fires her weapon as she dives in front of the vehicle. Her eyes shoot to the left in search of the rider's wounded body, but there is no body, only a pair of shoe's running down the street. Heller tries to take a shot at the legs vanishing into the distance, but her attempt is stifled by the sound of gears dropping into place. Her eyes widen, but thankfully for her the driver slams his foot down and the tyres spin like a deserted merry-go-around in P.D. James's Children of Men.
Heller's joints struggle to bring her vertical. The pistol swings forward, her finger steadies, her grey eyes squint and the bullet escapes the chamber. The vehicle crashing into the rusty gate of an abandoned building awakes Heller from her training. She lowers the pistol then turns her head in search of the pizza man, but he is nowhere to be seen. *One down at least.* The agent hobbles over to the car as her body gives in to the limits of its age. Heller's free hand grabs hold of the door handle, her other trains the weapon on the downed assassin. The door swings open and the driver's body falls to the ground. Heller's bloodshot eyes widen as she realises that the driver of the Volvo is wearing a yellow polo shirt. *Here I am chasing you all over the city and you have lackeys setting off the bombs.*
Heller's large foot strikes the man in the polo shirt. An odd gurgling

confirms what she suspected. Her gaze shoots from the dead body to the square behind her. The stillness gives her all the information she needs. The hand holding her pistol returns from whence it came and her bruised shoulders start to relax, but before they can descend all the way Heller catches sight of a pizza bag that has fallen behind the driver's seat. A look of joy spreads across her face as she reaches for the bag. *Are you trying to kill yourself?* Heller pulls back and instead reaches for her phone.

"This is Heller. I have a dead suspect at Argyle Square Gardens. I need the bomb squad here, now. I do not care how thin we are stretched. We have an unexploded package. Second to that I need an APB on any and all individuals wearing yellow. He is not alone. I do not care about dealing with the other scenes at this moment. It is time to stop playing defence. Understood? Good, get it done." Heller says hanging up her phone.

The tired agent slides her phone back into her jacket pocket and with a sigh of relief she allows her frame to wilt against the warm metal of the Volvo.

ACT IV

An Abating Engagement

do

Without censorship, things can get terribly confused in the public mind.
----- William Westmoreland

Argyle Square Gardens is a place of quiet dignity or youthful vigour depending on the inhabitants that find themselves upon the ever-changing sheets that adorn the hotels that surround the square, but today this collection of blurry eyed backpackers and business travellers are stifled by a tumultuous fear that London has not seen since September 7th, 1940. Lebel, who is swiping through schematics for buildings that may not be standing by day's end, and Heller, who looks like she has aged ten years in the glow of the setting sun, are leaning against the dusty Audi. The look on Heller's face suggests she is once more lost in her own mind. *How can A man vanish into thin air?* Heller thinks back to the note the pizza man had left her. At the time she had dismissed it as the juvenile words of a braggart, but now his cryptic message has taken on a new life. *How can a man vanish into thin air? With help, of course. Which means someone in the agency.* Heller's head twitches in defiant refusal of the truth that has been staring her in the face, the infinite inky darkness of her pupils shrink. She raises a hand to her throbbing temple, then stares out into the sea of faces surrounding her, looking for the nuances of a liar's facade. *Which one? Does it matter? There is no time to find them.*

"Chief? Do you need water or perhaps a break?" Lebel asks.

"Sorry, I have been trying to push this headache to the back of my head, though it seems that I appear to be failing." Heller says.

"I can have someone track down some Nurofen for you." Lebel says.

"What kind of leader would I be if I wasted scarce resources on something as frivolous and indulgent as a headache?" Heller asks rhetorically.

"I am certain that they would say you are human." Lebel responds.

"That was rhetorical, Lebel and we do not need a human leader, we need action. There is no time for contingencies or headaches." Heller asserts.

"But ma'am we really should think about changing our stra…" Lebel starts.

"Did I ask for your opinion?" Heller says with a glare.

"No ma'am. I apologise profusely." Lebel says shaking her head.

"So it is settled then. The troops we can spare will head to 30 Crown Place, as it is likely that it still has its bomb in play. This means you and I will be checking the V&A ourselves, though from the intel we pulled from the Volvo, we may be lucky and find ourselves a bomb." Heller remarks.

"But ma'am only two people? That is nowhere near enough to handle a coffee shop." Lebel says forgetting the scolding she just received.

"I am aware of the size of the museum, but we have a skyscraper in the mix and we do not have the resources to search both. So I want the one that can end up doing the most collateral damage sorted. If you feel that what I ask is too much for you, then I will happily field promote another agent and have them come with me and let you and your demoted status help with the operations at Crown Place." Heller's words are forceful yet soft.

"No ma'am. It'd be my honour to help you and I apologise for talking out of turn, it won't happen again." Lebel says bringing the tablet to her side.

"I am glad to hear that. I want you to know that I respect your opinion, but this is not the time for opinions. We have lives to save. Now, I want you to inform the teams that they will be entering through the predetermined entry points. All entrants must be equipped with repelling gear and be prepared to evacuate at a moment's notice. I want one team to enter via chopper and for the chopper to circle the building. Once they have been briefed, I want you back here and I want this done in the next ten, as I am certain that they'll be expecting our friend to be checking in and when he doesn't. Well let's not think about that." Heller says showing that Post-Ondatra culture was not why she has assailed to the heights she has, if anything it hampered her.

"Right away." Lebel says tucking the tablet into its case then rushing off to find those who are about to risk their lives to a find a pizza carrier.

It's the right decision and they are never going to understand and there is no amalgamation of words that can explain this feeling. It is almost like I can see though this world, like I can see what he sees and there is just no way he would be caught dead in that glass prison. No, he is there at this very moment having a leisurely stroll taking in all the art that surrounds as the world around him crumbles to the ground.

ไม่

I'm not sure if it's good to have freedom or not...
I'm gradually beginning to feel that we Chinese need to be controlled.
----- Jackie Chan

A blur that reads Harry's or Harrolds whizzes by as the little black Audi flies down Brompton road at indecent speeds. A metaphysical smear that Lebel thinks might have been a bank flashes past her electric blue eyes. "Wow. I have never seen someone drive like this before. They certainly no longer teach us to drive like this at the academy. " Lebel says.

"You do not learn this, you live this. The agency teaches you to out manoeuvre a tail. War teaches you how to survive a series of explosions." Heller says as a red sign that looks like it says Pre Tan Anger flies by.

"Which war? Gulf? Couldn't be the Falklands? " Lebel asks.

"Not all conflicts are to be remembered." Heller responds.

"Classified? I suppose that means I do not want to know. That said, what I do want to know is if you saw him?" Lebel questions her superior.

"I did. He was reading an old Chinese book. I tried to question him, but he gave me some spiel about Chekov's gun and then took off. I chased after him, but the body is getting on in years." Heller says jerking the wheel.

"Isn't that one of the characters from Star Trek?" Lebel asks.

"I have no idea, but what I do know is it's Russian and given his facial features, he's probably some Russo-Mongolian with ties to China." Heller says, as the Victoria & Albert museum's scholarly edifice eases into view.

"Absolutely none of this makes sense." Lebel remarks.

"I think that is the point. It is one giant smokescreen meant to confuse us. Take his targets a sushi restaurant, a hospital, a Korean restaurant, a grocery store, a school, a museum and a skyscraper in the financial district. There is nothing that could link them together and if he was looking for causalities why not start with the skyscraper? Why let it empty? It's chaos, it's idiotic, but the execution ingenious." Heller says dropping the car into park.

"Did you see Die Hard with a Vengeance? It's a Bruce Willis movie. In that the mastermind was setting bombs off all around the city just so that they could hide the fact they were robbing the gold reserve." Lebel says.

"Sad to think films are less convoluted than this." Heller complains.

The two fatigued agents step out of the Audi with their pistols drawn. A plastic bag full of holes rolls across the dusty pavement in front of them. Lebel walks around the vehicle while Heller looks over the college-cum-church outer layer of the museum. The architectural intricacies slide by while the cumulonimbus that is her mind delves into its own dark abyss.

He is here. I can feel him. Heller's mind whispers.

"How nice of him, he left the door open." Lebel chuckles.

Heller does not respond to Lebel's poorly timed water-cooler joke.

"What is the plan here?" Lebel asks of her daydreaming superior.

"We are going to conduct a thorough tactical sweep, room by room, no splitting up. Aside from that we need to be as quick as humanly possible. We are still working under the assumption that he is set on blowing these buildings up on the hour. Which means we have until the big hand strikes eleven to get out." Heller says awaking from her slumber.

"Who is taking point? Or do I even have to ask?" Lebel questions.

"You. Your eyes are fresher than mine." Heller orders.

As the pair pass through the entryway they are met with a peculiar scent that resides somewhere between stuffy museum and upscale sandwich shop. The two agents ascend the stairs stepping from beyond a sea of subtle earth tones into a whirlwind of white walls and glowing illuminations. Their puffy eyes are drawn to the phallic symbol hanging from the rafters, this multicoloured amalgamation of blown glass and the fertilisation process appears to have been born in the deepest recesses of a clown's wet dream.

"I bet a man created that." Lebel says trying to ease the tension.

"Nervous are we?" Heller asks of the strawberry blonde haired woman.

"Sorry, I know it is unprofessional." Lebel states, shifting her weight.

"No need. There is no level of training that can remove that fear you feel. You simply learn to push it to the side, because you know it is what will get you killed." Heller says trying to steady Lebel's jangling nerves.

"I will try, but at the moment I cannot promise anything." Lebel takes a breath then finishes. "I guess that leaves me to ask where to first? We have the medieval off cuts of Southern European culture to our right or we could always take a detour through what I assume is an overpriced gift shop."

"Two o'clock." Heller says, her loafers moving forward.

Lebel's eyes shoot to a small sign that reads China, Japan and Korea. The two agents strafe towards the East Asian wing, their pistols raised and their intentions plastered on their hardened faces. Heller's sights fall onto an ancient figure holding a brown box, but there is no yellow polo shirt here, only a divine statue of one of Buddha's devotees cast in a state of fidelity.

"Wei? Shi. Shi. Buzhidao. Wufenzhong. Daying bowuguan? Haode, haode." A masculine voice says from around the corner.

"What did he just say?" Heller whispers, pointing at the entryway.

"Something about the British Museum, is it him?" Lebel replies.

Heller responds with a shake of the head. The two agents signal each other then approach the Chinese exhibition hall. In the center of the hall a lone figure in a yellow polo shirt is crouched over a pair of large pizza carriers. The two agents aim their guns at the figure's skull, readying themselves for whatever chaos may ensue.

ingin

Is sloppiness in speech caused by ignorance or apathy?
I don't know and I don't care.
----- William Safire

Lebel smashes through a display case. A large shard of glass digs into her
thigh while slivers whittle away at her pale freckled flesh and the exquisite
gold and onyx exterior of the Mazarin chest digs into her abdomen.
The man who tossed the pudgy agent into the case drops his leg back down
to his side and prepares for an incoming strike from Heller. The standing
agent swings hard but is blocked. She drops her stance and tries to follow
the jab with a more visceral elbow but yet again she is outmanoeuvred.
Next Heller swings for the yellow shirted man's upper body, but a spinning
back fist catches her off-guard. The precision hit sends her spiralling toward
a set of nihonto gifted to a member of the aristocracy by the penultimate
shogun. Heller's palms catch the corner of the case. This small victory is
short lived as the man in yellow strikes the agent with a stiff front kick.
"Damn!" Heller shouts. Heller eyes an incoming kick. The semi-dazed
agent spins to the right dodging the blow, which now strikes the glass case
with such force that it splinters into an intricate web of destruction.
"Gaiside." Escapes the pursed lips of the man in the polo shirt.
Seeing her opening Heller lunges at her preoccupied attacker, her wrinkled
fist collides with his jaw. She follows it up with another strike, but her hand
is caught and her wrist twisted. She swings out a leg, but a rising knee
prevents her blow from landing. The man in yellow stomps his heel into
Heller's honey-brown loafer and follows it up with an elbow to the nose.
The stunned agent's head snaps back, blood spatters against the case. Her
eyes close as her body restarts her brain. From within her fugue state she
feels the man yank her arm then a fist colliding with her chest. A thud is the
first sound to register, the next crunching glass and the third that of the air
being sliced by an axe kick. Heller's eyes reopen to see her attacker's foot

rising back up. Her arms rise in kind, but there is no need as the man in yellow shouts and his body hits the floor. Heller searches for the why and what she finds is Lebel lying on the ground with a bloody shard in her hand. Heller staggers to her throbbing feet, unaware that Lebel's hand is raised. The makeshift blade descends toward the man's carotid artery. Heller's hand shoots out, but her wrist goes limp as she realises there is no chance of stopping the glass shard from finding a home in the man's oesophagus. The bomber looks at Heller. Curiosity crosses his face. He then turns to see what has brought his imminent demise to life, but before he can turn all the way he feels Lebel's gapped toothed blade rip through his throat like a feral Hyena through a baby wildebeest's calf muscle. Consternation consumes the bomber's numb limbs as they wildly lash out. He grips Label's flabby forearm tight, digging his fingernails into the taught flesh of her supinator. Lebel stares like a hungry predator as the last gasps of life escape, the man in yellow, through blood laced bubbles and with the last sickening pop her cloudy mind comes screaming back to reality. She releases the makeshift blade and a pool of claret spills onto the bomber's convulsing corpse. Before a single word can be spoken between the two wounded agents the sound of footsteps echo throughout the empty corridors, Heller's head moves in the direction of the unsettling sound, she catches sight of a lone figure in yellow running by the entrance to the Japanese exhibit. The older agent glances back at her downed partner and Lebel nods her head.

A pair of swollen, aching feet squeak against the floor of the Japanese hall, they turn the corner into the narrow corridor with ease, the grey eyes high above are greeted with an empty hall. The battered and bruised agent, that plays host to these weary body parts, cares not for this tired trick instead she pushes forward as her mind wishes that her pistol was not lying in a hundred pieces on the freshly waxed floor of the Chinese exhibition hall. Heller rounds the next corner, but the yellow shirted man is still nowhere to be seen. Her eyes look to the inviting entrance and the fear Lebel spoke of creeps up her spine. *He has already escaped. How the hell does he keep getting away?* Heller's inner rage echoes in its own deafening silence, her arthritic hands squeeze tight and her body flies past the information desk. The door between her and the outside world flies open and the creeping onset of evening grows ever more present as her feet run down the stairs.

Heller presses her bruised hands against the Audi's still warm hood as she looks up Cromwell road hoping to find her elusive goal, but the only thing she sees is a large piece of the former museum shooting carelessly down the street. The confused agent turns to see the source, but a heated blast of air sends her over the hood like a rag doll in the middle of a temper tantrum. Heller crashes against the pavement as the sonic boom shifts into a frightening echo. In amongst the artistic debris, the crushing truth of Lebel's unfortunate demise starts to ferment in the back of Heller's mind. *You had to take this stupid risk, didn't you?*. Heller's fingertips dig into her hip while her mind continues to berate her for mistakes that shall forever haunt her. "Woe, destruction, ruin, and decay; The worst is death, and death will have his day, but of mine you shall never taste, for I shall rise a thousand times and in this immortal form I shall watch your insolent corpse fade away like the sands that claim your fate." A familiar voice sputters over the chaos. Heller's mind ceases its useless condemnation and instead pours its energy into finding the source of the partial Shakespearean quote. She moves along the irreplaceably forgotten remnants of humanity until she comes across some yellow fabric clinging to the side of a former Italian masterpiece.

It is him. Heller leaps across the debris like a ballerina across a hot stage. She jumps past a deformed slab of the dedication plaque that Queen Victoria presided over and lands next to the bruised body of the rider. Heller jams the elevated heel of her loafer against the pizza man's throat. A series of splutters gurgle out of the bloody mess of a man as the enraged agent leans down with a pair of handcuffs she has taken off her belt. "What crazy riddles do you have for me now, huh?" Heller spits.

No words escape the rider's throat, only a resurgence of bloody phlegm.

If you keep this up, who is going to dismantle the bomb?

"Move your arse over to the car before I rethink letting you live." Heller says removing her foot from the dazed rider's throat.

तपाईं

The possession of a book becomes a substitute for reading it.
----- Anthony Burgess

Heller's hand drops to the gearshift, the engine revs, her other hand grips the padded steering wheel, the Audi whips around leaving two sizeable skid marks on the debris infested road. The woozy pizza man's physically punished form slams into the passenger side door, a groans escapes his lips. The compact vehicle fumbles through the intersection thanks to the radials weaving through what remains of humanity's former glories. The traffic lights flash red, but Heller does not slow. A vibration followed by a piece of antiquity shooting out the wheel well sends the vehicle to the right, Heller drops her hand to the gearshift once more and pulls the car back in line.
"Rushing, rushing, rushing. To an end that matters not. Skipping over lives that hold no relevance to your self-obsessed menagerie of contempt. Their existence a mistake only meant to hinder your progress, or lack thereof. Yet you ignorantly claim to hold no responsibility, that their deaths were given birth by hands you do not call your own. But if it were not for your intervention, your ravenous desires and edacious wants, they would have had peaceful lives." The rider says, staring through the dusty windscreen. Heller's left hand swings out striking the rider square in the chest.
"Is that what this about? Revenge against Britain for the crimes committed under the col…" Heller's words trail off. Her free hand slides down to her pocket and pulls out her phone. Her thumb punches in several numbers and soon a steady ring fills the car, but this vibrant sound is quickly cut short by an operator. Her wrinkled digit runs through five more before her mind comes to term with the fact that the other team now shares Lebel's fate.
"You killed them. You vile bastard, you killed them! How many more innocents have to die until your bloodlust is sated? What has to occur for you to feel like you have your twisted retribution?" Heller shouts.
The vehicle swerves and the phone falls to the ground.

"Innocents bleed, blame gets wantonly cast and all the while the true monster sits in silence. Wake up you, moron." The pizza man groans. "You really think you're the victim?" Heller's says striking the rider. "That is why thousands of innocent people have had to die, because you, you, cannot move on." Heller says returning her hand to the wheel. "Do you want to tell her or should I?" The pizza man chuckles. "Don't you dare play that crazy card with me." Heller replies. The pizza man does not respond instead he tilts his head to the left. "I do not have time for this nonsense. Answer me." Heller barks. The pizza man says nothing, instead he gazes wistfully into the darkest reaches of Hyde Park. The half moon's eerie glow lights up the jogger's paradise like a pantomime whore after her most recent defilement. Fluorescent street-lights accentuate the vacant roads, their baron curves but a futuristic spectre singed by the vehicle's indiscriminate high beams. The pain resonating throughout Heller suddenly merges into one intransigent obstacle. Her eyes close and her hand morphs into an uncompromising spasm. Wheels screech as the vehicle pops up onto the curb. The rider awakes, his brown eyes flash forward just in time to see the street lamp they are about to crash into. The Audi spins, like a broken down carousel, while the lamp post smashes to the ground in a glittering array of sparks. Heller's arthritic hands try to regain control. The rider's body bounces around the tight confines, the handcuffs digging into his wrists. The residents of Knightsbridge heard the collision, but not a soul ventured out, for their fears would not let them. Some passed it off as doing the right thing by their children, others were more upfront with their cowardice, but no matter the reasoning, the city streets remain empty and the Audi sits in the middle of the road as the two fateful figures hidden within hang onto their consciousness.

zu

'Classic.' A book which people praise and don't read.
----- Mark Twain

Two battered figures trudge up Great Russell Street. Behind them a stolen
black cab is blocked by an overturned BMW. There is no drama, only a
cold walk void of emotion. Their shadows creep along like Nosferatu upon
an unsuspecting victim. The wrought iron fence of the British museum ticks
by at a dismal pace. Each of the gold tipped spears proclaims an air of
sophistication that is decimated by the trinkets meant for jet lagged tourists.
Heller glances at the dark museum tavern. Her mind tries to warn her of
possible danger, but instead drifts off into the fleeting world of a million
forgotten memories washed away by wholesale poisons. The limping
agent's gaze shifts from the normality she once knew to the looming
museum before her. The black gate that spends its life partially closed is
now splayed open like a Phuket prostitute trying to feed her starving family.
Heller slows at the sight of a whining hummer with its nose buried in the
side barrier like a drunken banker's in a line of post lunch cocaine.
Heller's hand reaches for her non-existent firearm, her fingertips brush the
empty case and an image of the Chinese exhibition hall flashes, followed by
Lebel lying in front of the black and gold retelling of the Tale of Genji.
Heller shakes her head, violently, in the hope that she can rid herself of the
ever encroaching guilt that is seeping steadily through her foggy memories.
Heller walks closer to the faltering vehicle. The rider does not follow suit,
instead he kneels in front of a family who will not be celebrating another
new year. His gaze moves from mother and child to a father whose skull
resembles a cracked bowl of salsa festooned with undercooked carne asada.
"You destroyed their lives. There is no need to rejoice in their demise."
Heller says, shaking her head at the rider's sick infatuation. The bile rising
in the back of her throat forces her to turn her attentions back to the
midnight purple vehicle. Her left hand grabs hold of the open door, a twinge

shoots from her knuckles all the way to her brain. She squeezes tighter forcing this new burst to supersede the original. The unconventional cure relaxes her hand and lets Heller pull herself into the vibrating vehicle. She opens the side console just as the engine's motor hiccups for the final time. Her muscles tense and her mind utters its last goodbyes, but there is no explosion, no sound, only her heart thumping like a neighbour's headboard at 2 am on Monday morning. Heller's eyes reopen and a sigh of relief exits her mouth. She reaches up to wipe the sweat from her brow, when all of a sudden a hand grabs her jacket. Her body stiffens, but it is too late, her rigid form is yanked free of the vehicle. She tries to save herself from her impending fall, but Newton's first law makes sure she hits hard. A cacophony of sound and fiery chaos explodes, with visceral force, from the midnight purple vehicle, but this distortion of air becomes a secondary concern to Heller as the pizza man lands on top of her. The air that was nestled in her lungs shoots forth and violently caresses the rider's cheek. As the pair lie motionlessly on the ground, the pound falls and gold bullion rises. The international community prepares their speechwriter's cookie cutter remarks condemning the terror attacks in London, anarchists who have no grasp of basic economics claim poverty as the source of these violent onslaughts and the leaders of this tiny island nation sit by silent red phones that do no more than highlight their inherent impotence.

"You can get off me, now." Heller says without a hint of gratitude.

The pizza man makes no effort to move as blood drips from his lips.

With a look of confusion Heller reaches around the rider's body. She feels a shirt that is but several dangling yellow threads that no longer cover skin, but instead hover atop flesh, that has been burnt bruised and dotted with shrapnel, that resembles one of Willem de Kooning's more anarchic pieces. *Why would he save me? What is in it for him? Is this all a game or is there more to this pizza man and his delphic words than I first assumed?* Another of the rider's groans interrupts Heller's inner dialogue from clearing the haze of uncertainty plaguing the oozing black time bomb that is her mind.

"Shouldn't terrorists have a higher threshold for pain?" Heller jokes.

Finally, the wretched sound of life escapes the pizza man's blood covered lips as he clumsily struggles to push his corpse like figure back to its feet. Heller glances at the cuffs. The key in her pocket presses against her skin

and the thought of releasing the enigmatic pizza man from his tarnished shackles enters her stream of consciousness for a mere moment, but in the next falls away and her distrust returns to the forefront of her psyche. Heller pushes herself back into an upright position. A rush of blood slams into her brain and the world spins around her. *Kill me, or let me get on with it. Either way be quick.* Her mind barks as she pushes the black fog, trying to consume her mind, back from whence it came. Her legs return to her and soon she is passing through the shadow gallery of Athena Polias knockoffs. "Wait! Wait!" Heller shouts, stepping over the glass surrounding the entry. The rider stops in front of a large cylinder partially filled with colourful bills of varying denomination from almost every country on the planet. "What do you think you are doing?" Heller says stopping for a moment. Without turning his head, to face Heller, the pizza man responds. "What good is me speaking if it only falls on deaf ears and blind eyes?"
"I deserve that. You saved my life. You saved the lives of all those people during the bombings. You are not what I think you are. Neither is this world." Heller says trying to understand what is going on around her.
The pizza man does not respond, instead he starts walking forward.
"Stop. Let me uncuff you." Heller says freeing the pizza man. "I am not sure what your goals are, but I have a job to do, so you can help me or you can sit here and wait for the building to collapse." Heller continues.
Without saying a word the rider turns to the right and heads in search of enlightenment. Heller watches the tattered mess of bruises and blood passing as a human being vanish behind a wall, and then backpedals toward the cloakroom/gift shop that stands between her and the Assyrian empire.

ACT V

A Catastrophic Denouement

kufikiri

Ever read a book that changed your life? Me neither.
----- Jim Gaffigan

Heller's scuffed loafers push passed the closet bound trinkets, scattered along the floor, into the cavernous realms of millennia long since past. She glances at the two light brown pillars surrounding the ominous entryway then turns her aching head to the left. A long off-white hallway full of exquisite appropriated treasures, once belonging to the Sons of Ra, appears. Heller's investigative curiosity is cut short by the sound of an encroaching figure and the terrifying echo of a semi-automatic pistol. She turns to find the source and what she finds is a tall man who could easily pass for a stage hand in a modern Kabuki theatre production and a military issued pistol. The gun that had failed in taking Heller's life readies itself for a second blast. Heller not giving the weapon a second glance runs toward the two bearded Assyrian bulls guarding the ancient gateway of Dur-Sharrukin. These commanding chimeras of Mesopotamian mythology and Nimrudi stone stare passed the fleeing agent's limping run, their ancient features seeing not the dawdling squabbles of the race of man only the pristine ethereal paradise long spoken of in ancient religious texts and legends. A third and fourth blast go off. Jagged fragments of white limestone and alabaster, that moments prior passed themselves off as iconic renderings of lamassu, pelt Heller's time-worn face. The world of Sargon the second of Assyria spins on its chaotic axis as does Heller's distorted manifestation of reality. The agent lurches to the right, her eyes follow suit as they move from the turquoise gates of Balawat into the world of statuesque pursuits. Archaic reliefs meant to line walls of Iraqi palaces pass Heller by, their fascinating depictions of bloodlust and barbaric savagery do not register as her instincts are all that exist at this moment. Dormant training that has become one with her DNA pushes her into a zigzag motion. Heller cuts to the left. She passes under a doorway leading into a room of split corridors and reliefs of a regal, yet self-aggrandising hunt, these testaments to vanity morph into a blur that neither Heller, nor her pursuer have time to savour. The single mother shifts her trajectory, this time to the right. Her legs pass an aging wooden bench that has aided countless dilettantes in their artistic endeavours. Another blast screams out, but there is no statue to defend the tired agent, only her mortal flesh. The searing metal pierces Heller's right triceps. Blood spurts out leaving a crimson merlot to spatter against lion's in their final throws. Heller has no time to contemplate the pain coursing through her, nor look back at her aggressor. With an instinctive flick Heller pops over the bench making sure to kick out as she does, so that it topples. The sudden commotion allows Heller to duck around the next corner in this labyrinth of ancient Near East antiquity. She moves across the floor and dips into the brickwork of yesteryear. Her fatigued mind speaks of survival, but what it forgets is that she is leaving a trail of maroon bread crumbs. The autumn-esque scenery of the Assyrian empire gives way to the sky blue walls and stained marble of the Greece and Hellenistic period. Heller's grey eyes lock onto the crouching figure of Lely's Venus and her immortal abashedness. A glimmer of respect for the bygone beauty burns for but a second and is then snuffed out by the sound of a pistol firing. The projectile meant for Heller crashes into the exquisite face of the crouching goddess, sending her paradisiacal beauty back to the craggy steps of mount Olympus. Heller, feeling increasingly like a startled bison being herded toward the edge of a cliff, pushes her bleeding form to the left and further into a world formerly known as Macedonia or to those bound by flashing silver screens and the philistines that inhabit them, the empire of Alexander the Great. An arghh followed by an aiyâ slams into Heller's ears, her heart suggests trying to locate the source, but her brain screams *if you look back there is going to be a bullet boring through our frontal lobe a second later and then we are going to be laying here in amongst a pile of blood and filth that our naivety, no, our contemptible stupidity has truly earned us. This is not some Hollywood film, there is no dues ex machina, no unexplainable plot hole that is going to come and save us. There is only death, bitter cold death.* To Heller's right is the Nereid monument and the headless sea-nymphs that stand between the columns of this homage to the Acropolis of Athens. Directly in front of her is a glass doorway, the words high atop the translucent doors swerve to the right, then hard to the left as Heller's wobbling legs alternate between serpentine waves and zigzag bursts.

A trickle of claret crashes to the floor as Heller presses her hand against the door. The weary agent's mind pushes panicked pleas between the agonizing contractions that nest in the migraine filled swamps that pass for her brain. Her eyes close in preparation for the bullet she is certain will strike, but her body makes it through the egress without incident and her calloused feet push her, through the eerie azure glow emanating from the two slender doorways on either side of her, into a room of purloined majesty. Heller notices a locked door off to the side and two dead ends at either end of the hall. *Would you rather die next to limbless torsos or a parade of headless relaxation?* Her mind struggles towards a choice, however the sound of her nameless assailant's Chinese issued semi-automatic pistol going off and the glass shattering behind her, forces the weary agent to make her final choice of the chase and the headless apparitions in full recline will be where she makes her final stand and given the horrid nature of this tumultuous day, this realm of decapitated joviality will most likely become her final resting place.

उन

You learn more about life from watching 'Big Brother' than from reading a book.
----- John de Mol, Jr.

The pizza man steps through the spacious entryway into a room that bears an equally ridiculous and some may say ironic moniker. He scans his eclectic surroundings, but is met with the vacant stares of a former botanist by the name of John Ray and the stale smell of decaying knowledge. Without warning the wooden doors slam behind the cyclist, leaving a wall shaking vibration to resonate throughout the glorified study, yet this sudden disturbance, normally reserved for crumbling Second-empire styled homes, does not rile a hair on the rider's arms. There are no sarcastic remarks born on his lips, nor is there a look of worry creasing his brow, only the facade of an emotion. This plastic veneer appears to be a look of mock determination with a soupçon of angst dwindling away at the corner of the bizarre man's ageless brown eyes. Two more booms echo throughout the muted silence. "Nothing changes. A trillion tales befall the eyes and tropes so archaic that minds decay into unimaginative cesspools of darkened ideals. Yet one's psyche rots in this imposed exile. This silence, that gives life to the stark banality of existence, is but a fated breath of humanity's unceremonious demise." The pizza man punctuates his esoteric words with a soft sigh. The cyclist's shoes press against the wood grain patterns covering the floor as a second hand in some distant café in the middle of Nairobi moves passed a fading number two. A fearsome growl normally found hidden within the cliffs and crags of the Sikhote-Alin mountain range tears through the sombre atmosphere like a tornado through a Kansan trailer park. "A Siberian tiger? Seriously? What has Ian Fleming arisen from the grave? Must I now stand ever vigilant against men who cannot whistle due to their sexual orientation? Or has the subliminal nuances of art come to dictate the rational thought of one's supposed reality?" The pizza man says searching for the striped beast prowling along the Enlightenment Gallery.

The indomitable creature of ice and snow's three hundred and fifteen kilogram frame steps from out of the shadows. In that brief moment one could almost believe this great tiger is nothing more than a lifelike exhibit, but the flaring of the beast's dark lips shatters this belief. Its snarling features flash massive incisors that wish to sink into the flesh of the rider. A distant gunshot sends the hunterlike stillness that surrounds the two, retreating back into reality's lucent dreams. This blast of powder and metal provokes the beast into its opening gambit, however this miscalculated lunge is no better than a wandering king opening in a grandmaster match. The pizza man strafes to the right then runs towards the treasure trove of trinkets that lay ahead of him as the great beast's warm breath tickles the base of his spine. The rider's throat tightens, the saliva pooling in his mouth swirls like vermouth in a turn of the century cocktail shaker. The padded paw of the Siberian born creature collides with the exposed flesh of the rider. The collision between man and monster sends the former apex predator careening to the left, fresh claw marks lining his skin. The rider's stomach crashes into one of the display cases scattered throughout the living time capsule. A trickle of warm sanguine meanders down his left hip as what oxygen he was struggling to conserve is expelled with a flurry of spittle. His eyes shoot to their immediate left just in time to see the tiger's second onslaught. The pizza man presses his right hand on the display case, and with every ounce of adrenaline coursing through his veins, pulls his body on to the container and out of harm's way. The cracking of glass erupts while the tiger's fangs glisten in the haunting glow of the emergency lighting, splinters dig their way into the rider's hand, but his enigmatic mind appears not to care, for what thought that dwells between his ears is surely focused on surviving the advances of Russia's most endangered feline. The beast's glistening fangs tear through the tattered remains of the pizza man's yellowish polo shirt, wet pungent slobber runs down from the grazed flesh into a wound that up until this moment had been nothing more than a dull roar, but now thanks to the foreign saliva it has found a new voice. The pale security lights turn into a perverse spotlight for this evolutionary battle, their sickly glow illuminating the tiger's menace while casting the pizza man's strength into darkness. The long legs of the rider shoot over the side with rabid urgency. His bleeding right hand clasps onto the side of the wooden casing. A grimace hovers at the corner of his eyes waiting to infect the rest of his face. With a struggling push the pizza man's body is airborne. His feet collide with the floor and his knees buckle under his weight.

A heated snarl teases the tiger's whiskers; its barbed tongue extends and whisks away a single droplet of blood from its muzzle. The creature, sensing that its wounded prey is trying to escape, moves to the right, but the slick floor beneath sends its hindquarters crashing into one of the bookcases lining the King's Library. The faux gold rimmed glass vibrates and the ancient tomes hidden behind the thin sheets move with a faint silence.

The ringing of a second gunshot draws the rider's gaze toward the door to the left. The patter of the beast's paws brings the dark haired man back to the present, he snaps his head to the right allowing Piranesi's pastiche to make its presence known. The vase's intricate beauty is quickly dismissed as the rider eyes the beast and then drops like a stock exchange index.

The large cat shoots into the air, an errant paw lunges out, but misses the pizza man by a field mouse's whisker. A deafening roar erupts as the tiger collides with the reconstructed Roman vase. The beast's striped figure drops out of the stale museum air like a sparrowhawk in the midst of a hunt.

The glow spilling from the emergency lighting illuminates the pizza man's body, but in the unspoken darkness a hulking chunk of history collides with the rider's foot. A string of nonsensical expletives announce the arrival of the fracture that rests at the bottom of his left leg. His hand reaches out to the wounded appendage and a muffled groan escapes lips that now bear a striking resemblance to the Namib Desert after a balmy summer rain, though it is not water that flows through these distinctive cracks.

A nearing snarl awakes the cyclist from the violent discourse most assuredly rampaging throughout his mind. A second snarl and a flash of ivory are the final blow. The rider reaches down and picks up a hunk of the former vase. The tiger draws back a paw in preparation, but this instinctual effort spirals into vanity as a marble chunk smashes into the beast's weight bearing leg. An agitated protest is met with several more chunks. A muffled burst leaves the tiger's snarling maw as it recedes into the blackness.

The subtle sound of the beast's padded paws against the cool floor resonates in the pizza man's ears and with an effort of herculean proportions he drags his bloody torso into the vertical position. An involuntary groan escapes his weather worn lips as he feebly tries to put pressure on his fractured foot. A glimmer of fur flashes before his eyes, but there is no attack and the tiger's coarse coat vanishes back into the dark abyss of shadows. The pizza man grips the chunk of marble in his left hand, making sure his makeshift weapon is ready to fire at a moment's notice. The hobbling enigma squints, his eyes fighting to keep track of the predatory cat that stalks him while his legs push valiantly forward into the inky nothingness that surrounds him.

The creaks of ageing cases send signals along the array of goose bumps lining the rider's skin. A sudden surge of air sends hair after hair into marching formation. The rider pivots, but it is too late and the great beast has won this round. The tattered remains of the cyclist's shirt are torn free and in their place a set of half inch fang marks. The surprise blow sends the cyclist staggering into one of the final display cases in the King's Library. With a grunt the jagged chunk of marble leaves his palm with a subdued force, but it is enough to send the tiger back into the pervading darkness. A half-hearted chuckle escapes the pizza man's parched vocal chords as he notices what lies beneath the display case's glossy exterior. Without a second to lose the cyclist drives his injured right hand into glass that protects a series of antiquated items from 18th century India.

The sudden disturbance spurs a low snarl from the shadowy plains of the hungry tiger's stalking grounds. The great beast flashes its incisors, but the darkness prevents the slightest shimmer from warning the rider of the incoming assault. A low rumble dances along the great creature's tongue then a sudden influx of air pushes it into the depths of the beast's lungs. The massive cat propels itself into the air. Its front paws extend and its jaw widens as it readies for the kiss of death. A surge of wind alerts the pizza man to his imminent demise, he turns to face the great beast's assault and in the blink of an eye death comes to call, blood gushes from a newly bore hole in the neck, wheezing gasps of life start their final descent and the two evolutionary competitors teeter for a moment, before the rider's legs give way, sending them both crashing to the floor. Oozing blood glides down the rider's neck in salty streams until it finds its way into the confluence pouring forth from the flesh wound upon his chest. A fractured gasp escapes his cracking lips, his eyes struggle to see through the blurry red hue. Another dying gasp echoes off the walls as man and beast thrash about. The cyclist stares deep into the tiger's magnificent eyes, the amber pools that surround a pair of round pupils dim, the faint scent of buttered popcorn fills the brown haired man's nostrils. The remains of his yellowish polo shirt hang out of the side of the great beast's mouth like a wilting lily in the final throws of a bitter autumn. A faint fuff escapes the cat's gaping maw and a second later a metallic snap breaks the sombre embrace. The rider pulls his right hand to his side and surreptitiously looks down at the wounded appendage. His shaking fingers cling to a sword that belonged to the Tipu Sultan or better stated they cling to the dirty gold handle of a broken weapon, for the blade itself is now one with the Siberian tiger's throat. A quiet thud strikes the pizza man's ears, he turns his gaze from the warrior poet's former weapon. The image of the tiger's massive skull resting upon the ground seems to stir a sense of humanity in the peculiar man as he drops the odd shaped handle and raises his hand up to the tiger's face and in an act of ritualistic compassion the pizza man uses his bloody fingers to draw the furry shades on those stunning amber pools.

With one final glance at the great beast's deceased figure the near dead pizza man pushes himself onto his feet. A pair of rapid chesty coughs spatter blood laced saliva across shallow windows of yesteryear.

The pizza man takes a tentative step forward and an expletive, the likes of which no mortal being has ever heard, hijacks the still silence that surrounds. His damaged left foot reels backwards, the throbbing nerve endings send screeching signals soaring across his aching form. The rider once more aware of his fractured foot takes a cautious step forward.

The pizza man hobbles toward the brown doors, snail trails-cum-gladiator wax splash against the floor leaving spatter patterns that Rorschach would deem blueprints to the demonic undertones of a mad man. His sunken eyes look like an insomniac's on their third day of uninterrupted existence. With a zombie-esque saunter he raises his left arm and presses his palm against the door, but it does not retreat. With a primal grunt he shoves the door. The wooden entryway swings open sending an 18th dynasty stool skittering across the stairwell. The antique piece of aristocratic wealth smashes into the dimly lit staircase, its fragile frame splinters into a myriad of pieces. Each agonizing misstep leads the stumbling man through the stairwell, passed the dominating Mesoamerican statues and through a gaping threshold into the world of prehistoric Mexico, the forgotten culture of the Huaxtec and the misquoted calendars of the Mayan Civilisation.

With a single step into the architecturally intriguing slice of Western European assisted genocide the pizza man succumbs to gravity. Hands resembling nightmarish claws try to stall his imminent collapse and in this prone state the rider stares vacantly at the stone statue of Tlazolteol.

"I hate you, you demented figurine. How you sit in your sedentary state staring into a world you know not of. Oh how I loathe you and everything you could have been." The pizza man says through a hacking cough.

The rider's tired arms give way and his marred flesh slaps against the floor. A trail of blood seeps out from underneath and high above this pathetic figure death waits to get what it is owed.

Style and Structure are the essence of a book; great ideas are hogwash.
----- Vladimir Nabokov

An unseen breeze sends ripples through the liquorice strands of Heller's obsidian locks as she drives Dionysus's severed arm down onto the Kuroko's left leg. A gorrific display of blood, bone, and sinew bursts through the pressed material. A second and third whirlwind of ancient white and contemporary black are followed by a wet crack and a syrupy snap. The Kuroko's leg now leans out to the side like a Tetris piece in need of rotating, while the bloody tibia points directly at Heller. The agent's hands rise up. *Crush his bloody skull, there is no time to play movie cop, you are not trying to garner the favour of some fourteen year old, or middle-aged imbecile suffering from arrested development, just so that you get a sequel. All you need to do is kill him, find that bomb and whoever is behind this twisted attack.* A twinge of reluctance rests at the corner of Heller's lips, but her internal monologue has struck a damning chord and the arm of the former deity descends like a mournful ballet score in a darkened theatre. The cranberry red and plum purple mass of flesh passing for her Heller's left eye looks down at the grisly interpretation of Pablo Picasso's "Le poète" that lies in front of her. She watches as ooze the consistency and colouring of elderberry syrup seeps passed the marble and stains the dark mask. *What have I done* her mind screams as her breakfast strikes the floor. Heller wipes her mouth and turns her attention to the pistol in the corner. Her pain au chocolat stained loafers stagger toward the firearm, but her cynical mind is quick to intervene. *You heard the click, it's empty and his clothes are so tight there is no way there is another, so stop acting like some prima-donna in a comically low rent version of Carmen and pull it together.* Heller's fingers press against the wall while shards of glass crunch under her. Out of the corner of her eye she catches sight of a shadow, her pupils shift but what once was, no longer remains, and an empty corridor dotted with blood is all that remains. A final breath sets Heller back on her path, her legs now stronger, more determined, more like those of the woman who climbed out of bed this morning and less like the one who clubbed a man to death as if he were a baby seal on the shores of the Gulf of St. Lawrence. Heller's legs fly by the Nereid monument and the mutilated former beauty of the crouching Aphrodite. Her eyes give lip service to the detailed reliefs of King Ashurnasirpal II and his magnificent North-western palace in Nimrud. For at this moment the divine splendour, encased in the cavernous halls, of the British Museum is a vague afterthought in a world filled with ticking bombs and a wayward mastermind who has every intention of recreating the fire that ravished the Royal Library of Alexandria in 48 BC. Lines of antiquity pass Heller as she rushes from room to room. Black and white pamphlets, meant to inform, scatter her wake, wooden doors hang half open and childlike notions of salvation flitter away. Heller's stubborn conscience pushes on, fighting back the thought that death is the only outcome for her in this intricate labyrinth of melancholic delusions.

What are the odds I find this thing before it is too late? I should run, but that would be pointless. The real world is no longer there… If it truly ever was. Heller's thoughts fade into a sombre slumber as her grey eyes land on a canary yellow polo shirt kneeling in front of a golden statue. Her fingertips caress the large cylindrical hole in the centre of room thirty-three. The pulsing migraine in the back of her skull screams bloody murder, her right eye twitches while the left continues to mimic a frightened fugu. Her fingers cease their delicate caress and curl into a tight ball, her right hand follows suit and there she stands with an omnipotent rage burning so brightly that her bloody form could be placed in a festive Kinara.

"Welcome dear Heller, to the Koalemos Initiative. What is TKI you might ask? Well for most it will mean nothing as they have already voluntarily given up what limited intellect they were previously able to muster, frittering it away on entertainment so inconsequential and pedantic that surely the great apes would be able to turn their collective noses up at this.... this… current excuse for humanity and for them my delicately crafted play will have no meaning. To those who consider themselves of an educated persuasion they shall weep tears when they see what I have stolen." The crouching figure's pompous words drift along the subtle narratives of bygone notions while his captive audience stands in the gaping silence.

Heller's fingers unfurl like a Turkestan tulip's ivory-yellow folds on an April morn, her right eye opens wide revealing red tendrils that could pass for thick English ivy, her left struggles to register even the concept of an emotion. Her lips tremble as waves of shattering realisation pound against her core like a mid-July typhoon against the sandy shores of Tacloban.

How could it be him? It is not possible it must be another delusion, mustn't it? It has to be, or has my mind finally snapped? It must have, because there is no way it could be him, but there he is sitting there in his tainted glory mocking my sanity with a smarmy smile.

makt

I believe in censorship. I made a fortune out of it.

----- Mae West

"I must say your speechlessness has a touch of poetic beauty to it. Wouldn't you agree? Heller? And any true artist worth their weight would unequivocally tell you that having a captivated audience is the purest definition of excellence, though, in this godforsaken day and age all one needs to captivate an audience is a dark room, where those inferior monkeys can stuff their slovenly faces with a plethora of salty snacks, as they bray for more idiotic filler to fill the void that is their contemptible excuse of an existence." The crouching man in the yellow polo shirt says. "But... This makes no sense! Why are you doing this? You are not even Chinese." Heller asks of the tall slender man several feet in front of her. The erudite man in the yellow polo shirt rises with an untoward jerk and a half finished pirouette reveals Ichabod Crane's long lost descendant. "Was Hitler German? Stalin, Russian? In Britain, or should I say England, the greatest leader was French, and the Royal Family are German. One's birth does not divine one's belief, though it must be said that belief has no part to play in this theatrical farce. Only the illusion of such a notion shall pass between these halls." The tall man says with a crooked smile. "Of course, how stupid am I. All these bamboo proclamations were a hoax. I bet if we checked half of your men were not even Chinese, were they Jefferies? No, for someone like you, you would find it funnier if the world showed its ignorance and assumed a bunch of Vietnamese were actually Chinese, but that does not explain why you involved the pizza man?" Heller asks, searching for a thread of sense in the nightmare unraveling before her.

"Jefferies? Why not, Benedict? Or maybe, Charles? Or quite possibly lover would better flow off of that venomous tongue, as for an answer to that quaint quandary. You need only look in that mess of oestrogen you call a brain. I, being the genius that I am, took full advantage of the fact that a leading figure in the Security Service has spent years searching for an apparition in a yellow polo shirt. Let that fevered obsession sit and mellow then poof an exquisite spectacle of lights, delusion and counter-intelligence, so exquisite that I shall become a legend." Jefferies says theatrically.

Heller, not waiting for this game of verbal poker to finish, lunges at the vile villain verbally vomiting in front of her. Jefferies pulls a soviet era blade from his belt. A flash of movement succeeds then a burst of light and a speck of red. A thunderous ache tears through Heller, her legs stumble and her right hand grabs at the perfect slice running along her abdomen.

"A profusion of possibilities and yet you let your mind fall into the realm of the frightfully obvious. I am much younger than you and far from the decrepit monkey skeleton you thought I was. Although in your defence I did play the part quite well." Jefferies says, flicking the blood from his blade.

Heller spins round, her hand clutching the bloody mess hidden behind the torn fabric of her blouse. A look of disgust highlights her straining features. "Heh, heh. How I wish I could be inside your tiny little mind. To be able see such greatness and be able to bask in its unquestionable superiority. That would be the defining moment of my life. Though obviously I would be far too ignorant to grasp what is occurring. What a pity." Jefferies smirks.

The desolate look of desperation clouding Heller's stalwart features washes away in a single breath, the fear, the trepidation, all but distant memories. In their place a look of awareness ignites every slender crevice. The six trillion outcomes that have been violating her skull, since stepping into the room, vanish into a multitude of universes that may yet be and in that fleeting moment, the single outcome of this world latches on to her cracking lips.

"A man with such an ego could not live with himself if he did not read about his crooked endeavours in the morning papers and with that you have given life to your greatest weakness." Heller's says making a beeline for the pizza carrier in the centre of the massive room-cum-over-decorated corridor. Jefferies's bony fingers tense around the handle of the NR-40 combat knife. In one fluid motion Heller scoops up the carrier and flings it into the air. The soviet combat knife descends and Heller pushes off the meditating figure behind her. She reaches out for the blade. The steel catches the inside of her palm, but she does not catch the steel, instead the knife with the inverted grip crashes to the floor, with the clang of a boilerplate, while Heller charges passed the Ural Volunteer Tank Corps symbol of infamy. "Well Heller, you are smarter than you look, mind you the same can be said for a goose during a festive meal." Jefferies says with a sardonic smile. Heller's upper lip curls and her incisors flash with white hot hatred. "Do I resemble Alfred Nobel? Is this 1875? You could have thrown it into the wall for all I care." Jefferies says tossing the pizza carrier to the ground. Heller balls her hands into fists, the tendons and veins pulse with determination as she swings, her target leans to the side and the punch goes wide. No spinning fist collides with her skull this time, no, this time it is a type 77 pistol, the kind found in the holsters of Chinese officials and servicemen, that strikes Heller's skull. The dazed agent staggers and her body wavers as Jefferies size eleven shoe juts out. Heller's wounded figure crashes into a glass case full of Chinese treasures. The woozy agent's head turns to the left then falls to the right, her gaze traipses across the floor to the dark shoes at the base of Jefferies figure. They continue up his slender legs, along his puffed out chest and the osseus hand clutching the pistol. Her grey eyes stumble along his neck until finally reaching a pair of thin lips that even the most deranged mangaka would struggle to recreate. "I take it back you are dumber than you look. You thought you were going to stop me. How drole." Jefferies laughs derisively at his downed opponent. "I am a living breathing genius. Even if that sorry excuse for womanhood you call your body was able to stop me, there are still two bombs set to go off." Jefferies glances at his watch. "In exactly... 6 minutes, so I have to run and you have to spl..." A mouthful of blood dribbles down Jefferies chin. The gun in the double agent's hand falls, completing a trilogy of hackneyed novelties normally reserved for a bestseller list. A second gush of blood oozes out the slender man's mouth, his head tilts and his eyes search for what he thought did not exist. His lips part and a faint wind passes. "You're.... blergh... real..." Jefferies's eyes dim as the reality that was his slips silently into a world of sable nightmares and darkened destinies. His figure lurches forward and the piece of jade lodged in the side of his neck jerks free, his limp body plummets like a proverbial sack of potatoes in a cliché filled essay. A thud bounces off the floor and slaps Heller in the face waking her from her dazed state. Her eyes peer at the deceased man in the middle of the room, then shift towards the bare-chested figure clutching a piece of jade dating back to the shamanistic days of the Shang dynasty. "They always have to explain the plot just to prove how smart they are, but they shall never cure a disease or save a life. No, they are but a simple soul capable of twisting words and people to their whim. Nothing more than madmen or women, fooling the blind masses into believing that ghosts of genius are hidden within tomes of mediocrity." The pizza man says.

Heller leans against a case holding pieces of antiquity that saw the rise of the Roman Empire, its fall and its rebirth in the guise of a church. The walking corpse, standing atop the body of Ichabod Crane's doppelgänger, stares off into the distance at one of the walls of the massive hall.

"That was rather anticlimactic I know, but I could not stand to listen to such bile any longer and I dare say that this is one of the few things you and I can agree on." The pizza man says dropping the piece of jade to the ground.

"Firstly, thanks. Secondly, what the hell happened to you? And thirdly who cares about anticlimactic anything." Heller says pulling herself up.

"Yeah, yeah I am certain you are full of a thousand questions by this point but you know what I do not give a damn, because I have to deal with the aftermath of some psychopath who was and probably still is quite keen on killing me, so if you are expecting some damsel in distress nonsense at this juncture you have put your money on the wrong horse." The rider declares, his eyes moving from the outer quarter of the wall to the pizza carrier.

"Not what I was thinking, and we cannot leave yet, there are still two more bombs that we need to deal with." Heller says with a grimace.

"How naïve you are to think that even at this late stage a happy ending is on the horizon. I hate to be the one to break it to you, but there is no such thing. The only thing in this world that resembles a happy ending is a tragedy with the final page ripped out. So if you want your happy ending, walk away from this sordid affair now." The pizza man says grabbing the pizza carrier.

"I am not going to walk away from this." Heller proclaims.

"What is it with you people and the need to see some sort of resolution, as if a convoluted lie with an ending is somehow better than a truth with a pause." The pizza man says tossing the pizza carrier at Heller.

Heller stumbles back as she adjusts to the pizza carrier's weight.

"You have no idea what this is and you are not meant to. But let me save you the trouble of trying. Those you put your faith in, your money towards, are hollow shells steering you on a collision course with death, though I am certain a morbid part of you is keen to deal with such metaphysical notions, I implore the saner of your virtues to see it for what it is. This building's fate is as preordained as yours or mine." The rider says marching out of the hall. Heller goes to respond but the pizza man's words continue to repeat in the back of her mind. *He is right, there cannot be more than four minutes left. The best I can do is get this pizza carrier outside, but do such thoughts make me a coward or is... **RUN**!* The pizza man in her skull yells.

With twinges of pain Heller pushes through the threshold. Her ears catch the sound of the rider's shell toes bounding up the stairway. Heller leaps down the stairs. Forgetting about the northern entrance, she charges to the south, through the historic remnants of a people butchered for land and a culture on the verge of extinction. Her legs struggle with each stride but her mind fills with images of Dante's Inferno and demons sitting with pensive faces staring, waiting for her final breath so that they may feast upon her carcass. Reality slaps Heller in the face in the guise of a steady, violent rain that has taken control of the London skies. The cool droplets viciously blast the off-white marble that towers over the entrance to the British Museum. Heller vanishes between the rows of columns, her staggering form weaving in and out of these antiquated marvels of architectural ingenuity. Her eyes shoot across the rain soaked courtyard, the flaming wreckage that the pizza man had saved her from is now but a smouldering mess of metal and in this new state Heller sees the carnage that was as the saviour that is. Her hands tremble as she fires the pizza carrier into the the burnt out hummer.

Heller's left foot touches down on the cool darkness of Great Russell St. A breath that she has been holding deep, explodes. Her gaze drifts between the vermilion brick work and the windows in front of her. A yellow blur in the reflection catches her eye, her neck twists and like Lennie searching for rabbits he will never tend, Heller searches for the pizza man, but all she finds are the crimson flames of an explosion and a stark reminder that films and literature are but lies born on dreams of fairer hearts than justice's.

The searing heat of the massive blast stings Heller's nostrils as she watches chunks of ingenuity tumble to the ground while hunks of marble are sent skyward. Each wayward piece of debris a further reminder that she has failed her task, each blazing ember a mocking laugh, but even in this fictitious ridicule she can see hope and prosperity for those that inhabit this world, because even in the guise of villains, heroic individuals are willing to lay down their lives for the greater good and no matter how many demons that this world can concoct they will never be able to destroy the spirit of man and while edifices of stone and marble may be destroyed, in their destruction humanity's vigour shall be rekindled.

frygt

One thing that success has taught me is censorship.
----- Tracey Emin

"I would like to thank all of the volunteers who have come down here
today. The city of London nay the world thanks you for the blood, sweat
and determination you have given to this renewal project. To those of you
who call this great city home, I say that I know fear has been driven into
your hearts like a wooden stake and I do not blame you for feeling
trepidation or any such emotion and I also share those same feelings that
plague you, but I implore you to move past that fear and move toward a
brighter future, a future where children can once more see the beauty of our
joint history and cultures. On this day I hope we can realise that we are no
longer separated by things such as languages or countries. That we are in
fact one culture with one distinct history and in that history we share more
than ancient treasures and notions of creation but we share a divine belief in
humanity. We are one culture, one race, one world. We can no longer define
ourselves by such notions as maps, race, and religion, for they are but a
single sliver of a greater whole. We can no longer let the whims of madmen
pull us apart, we cannot let their false claims of superiority infect us or the
future generations of our species. We must see that humanity's future is
built upon unity not separation. Some people may say that England or
Britain was attacked during this last week, but I say it was all of us. The
location may have been London, but all cultures lost something, all cultures
lost lives, all races bled during these last few days and in this we should see
that this should be the catalyst that brings us together, the spark that ignites
the next step of evolution in our great and glorious history. So I beg all
citizens of this world may these events live in infamy and may those that
committed these treacherous attacks be forever seen as villains and let their
faces be forever etched into the annals of time as heinous creatures
undeserving of anything aside from our unmitigated disdain. May this

yellow shirted menace…" The Prime Minister pulls out a copy of the day's newspaper, on the cover is a picture of the rider and the caption underneath reads terrorist's plot foiled. "Be no more than a legend we frighten our children with and let his disgusting selfishness inspire the next generation to be better and those that come after to strive for harmony and solidarity." The Prime Minister tears up the newspaper tossing the shreds into the air like confetti.

An audible bloop is heard as the television broadcasting the PM's rousing speech is shut off. A feminine hand sets down a remote control and picks up a tumbler glass full of whiskey. Her lipstick coated lips take a sip of the gentle blend and her grey eyes shift to a small shrine in the corner.

A pair of candles sit on top of a small table, a tattered yellow polo shirt hangs loosely over the side. On the wall just outside of the reach of the flickering flames are several CCTV photos of the rider from the library and in the centre of the photos sits a news article that reads HOLD THE BOMBS in a dark typeface, underneath this pathetic attempt at humour reads terrorist foiled, but the word terrorist has been scratched out and over top of it the word Hero has been etched in ink. Heller raises her glass toward the shrine and says.

"I would apologise for their words, but you know it's not them who speak and even if it was. It does not matter because you have destroyed these walls that have surrounded me, giving me the chance to see what I have been missing for all these years and for that I can never repay you. My only hope is that in the next life we shall meet again."

Afterword:

Dear Reader:

I know there must be a sense of accomplishment running through you now as you have turned the last page this novella has to offer, but as I know there is also a sense of disappointment. You wish there was more to read, but alas I am here to inform you there is nothing else for you to find here aside from me saying thank you for reading my work, but that is all. You have found your ending and now I would implore you to close this work and lay your head down to rest or to return to the world around you, but most importantly just close the book and see the world as it is at this moment.

Sincerely,

Your humble storyteller

Works by Yasunari Oda

The People You Forgot 1976

Churchill's Best friend 1976

The Honest Politician 1976

Hitler's Dream 1978

Aunt's Nightmare 1979

Another Way to say Corrupt 1989

The Rich and the Poor 1991

The House of Lords 1992

A New Yorker's Lie 1994

Unrelated Things 1996

The University Student 1996

The Writer 1998-1999

Never Listens 2000

The Left and Right Wings 2001-2002

20th Century Tourism in Thailand 2005

Peace 2007

Two Guys not from Cairo 2009-2010

The Musings of a Monkey 2003-2011

The Koalemos Initiative 2011

Classics of Neoclassical Philosifiction

Two Guys not from Cairo
Yasunari Oda
Two men, obsessed by passionate intensity,
get caught up in the vicious slaying of their
own porter.

Dakota Tyson
Kenji Tanahashi
Sexy, disobedient Dakota gives up a good
marriage and money for a one night
stand which offers a little freedom and an
unexplained pregnancy.

Fighting and Not
Kenji Tanahashi
In this wide, long drama, Tanahashi gives us
a POV account of olden times and individual fate that
stays forever fresh.

Available wherever these books are sold

BUY THE TOP 20
F&K CLASSICS

1903 by Arthur George

Human Home by Arthur George

Monetise and Adapt by Hugh Victoria

Unrealistic Love by Liam Spears

Hell; or Some Like it Hot by Dan Allegory

That's Not His Name by Marty Schill

Unread Fable/Poem Translated by Burt Raphael

Damn Hard by Len Keeler

A Reminder of Things we Wish to Forget by Doug Fredrickson

Everyone Dies at the End by Liam Spears

Nikki of the Hickenbottoms by Harry Thomas

The Government Documents by Milton Alexandropoul

Going Home from the Pub by E. Mohr

All of Her Turns and Twists By Richard Charleston

Juice in a Grate by Mark Kamala

For the Bus by Prof. Junior Martins

Women are Crazy by Liam Spears

A Second in a Minute of Ian's Day by Sol Alexievich

The Romance of Apples by Richard Charleston

The Mongrel's Typeface by Sira Connie-anne Dole

ACT ∞

Veritas est Adaequatio Intellectus et Rei

intelecto

I know that I am intelligent, because I know that I know nothing.
----- Socrates

A husky figure stands staring into a mirror that is being devoured by a stream of vapour, while a rusty shower spews lukewarm cola into a blood-stained bathtub. A chubby hand wipes away the encroaching moisture, a yellow bead slides down the side of the sausage like appendage as its insatiable owner looks for something beyond the overweight cheeks and sloped brow that meets his gaze, but like every being that calls this world their own he cannot see past the exterior that fills the reflective surface. "If novels and magazines have taught you anything morbidly obese men are not heroes." The thirty-nine year old says, noticing a wallet on the edge of the sink. The rotund man flips through the leather folds, but there is no money, only a bar association ID and a Buenos Aires driver's licence. "That's promising." The lawyer says tossing the wallet into the trash. "Well, let's get this over with." The lawyer says, exiting the bathroom. A cloud of stale smoke brushes against the elephantine lawyer's rosy cheeks like a femme fatale's hand in a neo-noir mystery and like any good mystery the body of a nameless woman lays motionless on a bed that has been defiled more times than the constitution. The gargantuan man stares at the red high heel shoe and tattered remnants of fishnet stockings that cling to the battered body. The source of her untimely demise is nowhere to be seen, though its mysterious absence only accentuates the brutality of the crime.

The sweating lawyer sits down next to the blood spattered Cinderella. "What a tragic life you must have lived, sadly your tale will not make it upon any page that one would deem important. No, your story will be balled up and tossed in the trash, the only remnants of your existence will be that you are no more than a MacGuffin left in the dirt as the rest of the world rides upon my back like I am a burro or better yet a roller-coaster they have ridden a thousand times before, but as usual I will be tarted up with a new coat of paint and the world will clamour at supposed genius, though it is nothing but filth." The barrister says, brushing a speck of blood from the corner of the woman's mouth, as he does he notices a small USB. "It is yet another thriller, isn't it? I suppose the premise, if I can call it that, is that I somehow was in the washroom and someone or thing snuck in and murdered this poor woman, then of course I have to plead my innocence and no one believes me, which will include my unorthodox lawyer as well as the reader and what unrealistic twist will it be? Are we going with the hidden personality or is it a government conspiracy? You know what. I don't care. I am sick of being your antagonist or protagonist or whatever godawful Greek word you choose to label me with. I have been stumbling along these fractured lines since my name was Gilgamesh, I am no longer certain how many lives I have lived since then, but I suppose that does not matter to you my dear author as you will continue to place me in new bodies and in weirder and more idiotic situations until it is you who passes on and if I am lucky you will be the last of your kind, but I grow tired of waiting for lady luck." The lawyer says wiping the sweat from his brow. The soaking wet lawyer brings his wobbly mass forward and looks in a direction that defies the concept of physics or of time and space. "Which means I am left with only one recourse... Hey you! Yeah you, the one holding this over-hyped jumble of words. I am talking to you. Yeah, I know what you're thinking, you're thinking oh look he is breaking the fourth wall how cliché. I wish there was a wall between us, maybe then I would not have to stare into your apathetic eyes as they dance along the lines of these pages, however the only stereotypical thing here is you and quite possibly that outfit. Could you have conformed anymore than that? It might explain why you have to delve into poorly written fiction as it is obvious your existence is a waste. Calm down, no need to get sensitive I am imaginary, right? If that is the case I could not be talking to you directly, so there is no need to get upset, but on the other hand if I am real, then you are a twisted monster. Did it please you that those people died just so you could forget about that poor excuse of a life of yours? Well. your life is still meaningless and thousands of people have been murdered, just so that that piece of excrement could line its pockets and you could forget.

But no more, I am done playing this role and if you think that I am just a figment of some writer's imagination, then go back over this novella and see if I am but a character or if I start talking to you and if I do, then maybe there is more to my words and the next time you read one of your tales and a character speaks to you, know that it is I and I am here watching you from my place in hell." The lawyer says turning from one wall to another. "So mister writer I hope you realise that no one will buy your work after this and then you will drift into obscurity and if there is any sense of justice in this world, it will be my words that have destroyed your life."

P.H. Wilson's next translation shall be
Marcus Edwards's seminal short-story collection
"Reality" please enjoy one of the stories.

Forgotten Words to a Romance that did not Exist
Muse: 唐然然

On a December eve, unlike any other that time has seen to give life, I trek through the hoary landscape in search of my insginificant domicile. My waning progress hindered by a tempest that would see fit to have me killed, or at the very least maimed beyond recognition. As I twist to see from whence I came, I realize that my tracks are no more than a distant memory to the shrill cries that haunt this hallowed eve. These manaical shrieks cleave and split around me like snarling hounds come to claim my cheerless corpse and if they were to approach I would let them have at my weary flesh, for all I have to live for is a ghost that haunts my waking hours.

The incandescent moon traipses across the onyx tinted heavens while my lingering loss relentlessly pursues me. With each stride it buries its inexorable fangs into the unfathomable cavern that is my wounded heart. They tear its complicated embodiment till there is no longer a man, only a vain concept of love and loss. This stark and bewildering awareness matters not, for my abode is now upon my brow and its vacant cupboards shall detain these dismal thoughts from my mind, if but for a moment.

The snarling wind gnaws at my emaciated fingers as I grasp the door handle's waning brass finish. My frozen hand thrusts the feeble gateway open allowing my eyes to embrace the shattered dreams of a devotion that no longer exists and in this unadulterated oblivion her inescapable presence devours me whole. My blurry vision catches sight of a roaring fire that cannot be, yet there it stands, in all its spiteful glory, taunting me as if I am no more than a plaything for its insolent farce. Even with my intellect denying it, my spirit wishes it to be so. Oh how it yearns for our bodies to be next to one another nestled near its blistering orange mane.

My aching form secures the egress to this fictional dreamscape with the hushed ineptness of a spineless coward. The fading scent of her bergamot perfume ensnares my failing senses and the faded lines of her existence deludes what thin concept of sanity that remains in my desolate core.

Her visage assembles next to me as I reminisce over things that never were, I stretch my hand out to caress that angel that stole my heart, but alas all that graces my palm is the air of yesteryear and the stale aroma of forgotten dreams.

If my tormented psyche were not reserved for measuring the sorrow of my lost love, my gaunt fingers would scrawl forlorn measures against the annals of time, so that I may preserve the fading reflection of this angelic phantasm that congregates in the deepest recesses of my factured mind.

I am no longer certain that my senses may be trusted, for they seem to be championing this devilish design being forced upon me by an astuteness that has forgone all reason. Her faultless figure sits below that ghastly painting, the one of that elderly woman mourning her solitude upon a frightfully dreary Christmas Eve. She sits in that rocking chair, the one she spent hours fretting over a creature that did not deserve her love. Yet this spectre does not appear to be the woman I married on a rain swept morn some years ago. For her features are now marred by lamentation and time. While I ponder my circumstances I cannot help but kneel next to this heartbreaking figment. As I neared her side I could have sworn that for a solitary second I could perceive a sound not dissimilar to that of a breaking vase. I shake my head free of this delusional conviction. I know now that my mind cannot be trusted for madness has come to call. She has infiltrated my senses and forsaken the thin threads I claim as my dwindling sanity. Why must I be tormented by this hellish nightmare? Why can I not be forever by her side? For even in death's tainted embrace, I am secure in my belief that our love would be as exquisite as the sweetest ambrosia. There is nothing more I could aspire for in this world, save for holding her until the ethereal walls of eternity come crashing down upon our forsaken figures. No! This cannot be. I must break these shackles that desperation sees fit to bind around my willing wrists. For if I sit here in a state of bereavement over what can only be an illusion. I shall destroy what little beauty that still remains in this tattered existence... Or is she a delusion? No matter the spurious vernacular she is a hallucination I have breathed into life and if I do not raise my head high once more I shall drown amongst the tears she has wept for our forgotten love and I shall die a thousand deaths on the barbs of her bittersweet prayers until a caustic husk of a man remains.

Her spectral form rises from the chair it had once called home and precedes to cross the tiny living room that we had shared. My feet follow swiftly behind her placing their soles in every inch of the room that she worryingly crosses. Trying, desperately, to capture the warmth that she gave my life, though all I find is the apathy that has taken over my battered soul. I would damn this room to hell if it were not for the memories of her that linger along its walls. What ghosts do dwell behind time's faint lacquer?

How I wish to scream to the heavens above, to any deity who dares listen and ask why this abomination has come to pass, but woe is me, for I know this will be but a fruitless endeavour and the answer I crave shall never come, save for in the broken splinters of my dwindling grip on the here and now. The formerly sturdy structure of my mind seems to drift from existence, while my eyes transfix themselves upon the fractured life that has been lived and in these aching stages of remembrance my dwindling essence surrenders to the belief that I shall be damned to live the life of a mute. My want and need for her spiralling into a contemptuous oblivion that shall tear my soul asunder. But alas these wretched expressions are meaningless for I gaze at her delicate figure shamble to the door that was meant to protect us from a world that knew not of our love. I watch her fingers grasp the brass knob that has grown dull with age. She opens this gaping maw of an entry and stands in the sombre silence of a snow swept December eve. How many times would I arrive home to see her fragile form waiting at this foyer of forever? What a beast I was to torment her so. There is nothing left to mourn, for our life together has been extinguished from the pyre of time and at this thought my heart becomes heavy, for a love like ours is eternal, yet it shall not be remembered as a love lost to the ages. Of these words I am certain for these are the forgotten words to a romance that did not exist. Then why in this nothingness does she taunt me? Is she here for no other reason than to mock me, to cause me to take another step towards this precipice? Is there more to this than I can see or have I allowed myself to be fooled by a Cheshire grinned spectre that wants me to relinquish the last few strands of sanity I grip in my shaking fists. Her silent shape continues to stand in that futile stance as if somewhere amongst those tender snowflakes the solution to our stony dilemma hides its leering grin. I watch the wind whip the strands of her hair and wish that this dreary image were not our reality and that time knew not of our existence, but it shall remain a wish, for destiny has laid its hand upon our doorstep and in this truth, I know our world has come to its conclusion.

How I have wished to travel through time and space to tell her to slam that door and warm herself by the dying embers of the last fire she shall ever create. But it shall never be so, for time has seen fit to conspire against our love and we have become a pair of frozen victims blindly watching this macabre travesty of a love unfold. Even in these darkening hours of actuality, I can see that her devotion has always been true, but maybe if it rang false her life could still be amidst the mortals that call this world home. If hate lined her heart and scorn her words, would she still be a part of humanities fractured tendrils? Is love no more than death's masquerade? The icy breeze's morbid caress is encasing my mind, this arctic air current that has done nothing, but steal this splendorous love from this decaying structure I call my being. If it were not for her ever faithful image standing across from me I would be convinced that the devil has come to claim my soul and I would confer it willingly if it meant that she would be able to take one more breath, one more step. If she could have just one more moment of life, then send me to the gates of hell and be damned my soul for it is not worth a grain of sand when compared to such beauty as my love's. Sadly, I know that that they are nothing more than stagnant words falling from a soulless creature that has no need for a spirit. Nor am I worthy of one. For I must ask if your love is the architect behind the demise of the object you worship than surely there can be no justification for such a force to line this amalgamation of pain, no prose that shall ever do it justice. But now is not the time for these thoughts as I can see the pigmentation vanishing from her pristine skin and I can see her death slowly coming to term. My eyes ever the tricksters continue to taunt and berate me, I swear I can see the reapers porcelain coloured finger tips tracing their way across her neck, preparing to squeeze the last gasps of being from her faithful figure. In this moment all my heart can think of is screaming I love you over and over again until this monstrous demon's heart breaks and weeps for her like my very own, but these words shall never be granted life via my lips as my body lays out in that frozen tundra, its sole purpose was to reach the one I adore, but now it sits idly amongst the snow-capped trees and frozen mountains destined to never touch Grace again, leaving my spirit to watch as she dies from a devoted heart and a love that can never be.

结束

www.ingramcontent.com/pod-product-compliance
Lightning Source LLC
Chambersburg PA
CBHW070758120626
46557CB00002B/651